Leapfrog Press

P.O. Box 505 · Fredonia, NY 14063
(508) 274-2710 · leapfrog@leapfrogpress.com
www.leapfrogpress.com
Media contact:
Lisa Graziano, 508-274-2710, leapfrog@leapfrogpress.com

STEALING INDIANS
a novel
John Smelcer

1950: Four Indian teens from different regions of America are forcibly taken from their families and shipped to a faraway boarding school where their lives will be immutably changed by an institution designed to eradicate their identity. And no matter what their home, their stories are representative of every story, every stolen life. So far from home, without family to protect them, only their friendship helps them endure. This is a work of fiction. Every word is true.

"A poignant story of colonization and assimilation, something I know a little bit about. A masterpiece."
—Chinua Achebe

"When it comes to re-visioning the Native American experience in American history, few are as triumphant as John Smelcer."
—Howard Zinn, *A People's History of the United States*

"Smelcer captures the complexity, the pain, and what the meaning of the boarding schools was for not just the generation before us, but all of those that have followed. Its ripples are still being felt and suffered from in Indian Country."
—Joseph Bruchac (*Our Stories Remember* & *Jim Thorpe: Original All-American*)

"One of our most brilliant writers, John Smelcer tells a harsh truth about American history."
—Roxanne Dunbar-Ortiz, author of *An Indigenous Peoples' History of the United States*

Savage Mountain (Leapfrog Press, 2015)

"Set in the interior of Alaska, this novel balances family dynamics, brother-bonding, and high-stakes adventure.... The mountaineering and Alaskan drama is both realistic and exotic, suspenseful, and exciting. . . . Extreme adventure sequences and the strong brotherly relationship make this a solid general purchase."
—*School Library Journal*

Edge of Nowhere (Leapfrog Press, 2014)

Chosen for the 2014 **Battle of the Books** by the Alaska Association of School Libraries
ABA's ABC Best Books for Children

Leveling: Common Core and Fountas & Pinnell Guided Reading levels by Read-Ability

"A spare tale of courage, love and terrible obstacles . . . a novel that may have special appeal to teens who like to wonder how they would do if they had to survive in the wild."
—*Wall Street Journal*

"Smelcer's prose is lyrical, straightforward, and brilliant. This is an example of authentic Native Alaskan storytelling at its best. . . . The excitement and fast pace of the action are reminiscent of Jack London stories. This novel would make a versatile addition to any secondary English or multicultural curriculum. Not to be missed."
—*School Library Journal*, starred review

"More psychological depth than Robinson Crusoe."
—**Frank McCourt**

"Brief, thoughtful, and often lyrical, this is a quick pick for young teens who have the good sense not to confuse a short book with a shallow book."
—*Bulletin of the Center for Children's Books*

"With metaphoric elements and emotional catharses, the newest novella from John Smelcer . . . deliver[s] a unique survival story set in Prince William Sound in the Gulf of Alaska. . . . *Edge of Nowhere* is a survival story, but one with a strong heart."
—*ForeWord Reviews*

"Smelcer gives readers a crash course in Alaskan history, geography, and lore in a survival story that pits a teenager against nature's indifference. . . . A thought-provoking and moving coming-of-age story."
—*Publishers Weekly*

"A riveting, picturesque, trial-to-triumph tale. . . . Smelcer encapsulates the Alaskan landscape with the sheer authenticity only a Native could deliver…. Smelcer's interweaving of Alaska Native language, legend, anecdotal folklore, as well as local history throughout, makes…for an engaging [and] highly informative read. By way of remarkably poetic storytelling, [he] draws a flawless parallel between the unrelenting strength of nature and the indefatigable determination of the human spirit. *Edge of Nowhere* . . . is yet another gripping literary triumph for Smelcer."
—*Midwest Book Review, Reviewer's Choice*

Lone Wolves (Leapfrog Press, 2013)
"A beautiful and moving story of courage and love."
—**Ray Bradbury**

"An engaging tale of survival, love, and courage."
—*School Library Journal*

"Having penned over forty books, Smelcer years ago established himself as a rock star of Alaskan literature. But with this inspiring young adult novel . . . he promises to further solidify his status as 'Alaska's modern day Jack London.' . . . Showcases Smelcer's stylistic mastery of metaphor and simile, devices he flawlessly employs throughout the book that evoke the Alaskan landscape and provide much of the novel's richest detail. . . . Despite the gravitas of the very serious issues she confronts, Denny's is an inspiring and hopeful story."
—*Mushing* **magazine**, review by Suzanne Steinert

"Smelcer ambitiously juggles several themes, mainly tradition versus modernity and the importance of preserving one's cultural heritage. . . . [He] puts great care and detail into his depiction of traditional customs and daily activities as well as the current issues that plague the young people of these isolated communities . . . [and] adept focus on Denny's coming of age and the illuminating glimpse of Native Alaskan cultures."
—**Horn Book Blog**

"Powerful, eloquent and fascinating, showcasing a vanishing way of life in rich detail."
—*Kirkus Reviews*

"Smelcer's work has a touch of the classical, combining good old-fashioned adventure and survival themes with heart-tugging moments of clarity and poignancy that recall Jean Craighead George's *Julie of the Wolves*. Filled to the brim with letters, poems, and cultural lessons, this fascinating account passes quickly, much like the race itself, and brings the ultimate truth that triumph isn't necessarily about winning."
—*Booklist*

"A vivid tale which draws the reader into the harsh, yet compelling, beauty of the North . . . connecting to the younger audience with contemporary issues. A refreshing read with a charming and youthfully mature protagonist . . . a compassionate

and inspiring tale which highlights the importance of family, community, and heritage."
—*Midwest Book Review*, Reviewer's Choice

The Great Death

"The simple, lyrical language enhances the stark beauty of the winter setting. . . . The authentic details of survival in the winter wilderness are fascinating and should draw in reluctant readers."
—*School Library Journal*

"A gripping and poignant survival story. . . . Smelcer's prose is clean yet rich; original yet unpretentious, and he provides more than enough detail to satisfy diehard survival-story junkies."
—*Horn Book Review,* starred review

"This grim tale of the sisters' struggle against the elements will leave readers wanting to know more about this little-known time in history."
—*Booklist*

"With a prose style by turns informative, poetic and graphic, Smelcer tells of the sisters' journey away from their Alaskan village, a story of strength and courage. . . . An engaging tale of survival."
—*Kirkus*

"A classic survival story."
—*Bulletin of the Center for Children's Books*

The Trap

"Readers will be clinging to the pages of this graceful, haunting story. . . . How rare to find lyrical writing combined with real suspense. . . . Equally memorable and enjoyable for children, teens and adults. A small masterpiece."
—*Kirkus*

About the Author

John Smelcer is the poetry editor of *Rosebud* magazine and the author of more than forty books. He is an Alaskan Native of the Ahtna tribe and is now the last tribal member who reads and writes in Ahtna. John holds degrees in anthropology and archaeology, linguistics, literature, and education. He also holds a PhD in English and creative writing from Binghamton University, and formerly chaired the Alaska Native Studies program at the University of Alaska Anchorage.

His first novel, *The Trap*, was an American Library Association BBYA Top Ten Pick, a VOYA Top Shelf Selection, and a New York Public Library Notable Book. *The Great Death* was short-listed for the 2011 William Allen White Award, and nominated for the National Book Award, the BookTrust Prize (England), and the American Library Association's Award for American Indian YA Literature. His Alaska Native mythology books include *The Raven and the Totem* (introduced by Joseph Campbell). His short stories, poems, essays, and interviews have appeared in hundreds of magazines, and he is the winner of the 2004 Milt Kessler Poetry Book Award and of the 2004 Western Writers of America Award for Poetry for his collection *Without Reservation*, which was nominated for a Pulitzer. John divides his time between a cabin in Talkeetna, the climbing capitol of Alaska, where he wrote much of *Lone Wolves*, and Kirksville Mo., where he is a visiting scholar in the Department of Communications Studies, and is creating a new Native American Studies program, at Truman State University.

STEALING INDIANS • John Smelcer
200 pages • ISBN978-1-935248-82-8
Trade paperback, $13.95
Young Adult
August 2016

Published by Leapfrog Press LLC
www.leapfrogpress.com

Distributed to the trade by:
Consortium Book Sales & Distribution
www.cbsd.com

Books by John Smelcer

Fiction

Savage Mountain
Edge of Nowhere
Lone Wolves
The Trap
The Great Death
Alaskan: Stories from the Great Land

Native Studies

The Raven and the Totem
A Cycle of Myths
In the Shadows of Mountains
The Day That Cries Forever
Durable Breath
Native American Classics
We are the Land, We are the Sea

Poetry

Indian Giver
The Indian Prophet
Songs from an Outcast
Riversong
Without Reservation
Beautiful Words
Tracks
Raven Speaks
Changing Seasons

STEALING INDIANS

JOHN SMELCER

Leapfrog Press
Fredonia, New York

Published in 2016 in the United States by
Leapfrog Press LLC
PO Box 505
Fredonia, NY 14063
www.leapfrogpress.com

Printed in the United States of America

Distributed in the United States by
Consortium Book Sales and Distribution
St. Paul, Minnesota 55114
www.cbsd.com

First Edition

ISBN: 978-1-935248-82-8

Library of Congress Cataloging-in-Publication Data

Names: Smelcer, John E., 1963- author.
Title: Stealing Indians / John Smelcer.
Description: First edition. | Fredonia, NY : Leapfrog Press, 2016. | Summary:
Four Indian teenagers are kidnapped from different regions, their lives
immutably changed by an institution designed to eradicate their identity,
and without family to protect them only their friendship helps them endure.
Identifiers: LCCN 2015046700 (print) | LCCN 2015050716 (ebook) | ISBN
9781935248828 (softcover) | ISBN 9781935248835 (epub)
Subjects: | CYAC: Indians of North America--Fiction. | Kidnapping--Fiction |
Friendship--Fiction. | Identity--Fiction. | BISAC: JUVENILE FICTION /
People & Places / United States / Native American. | JUVENILE FICTION /
Historical / United States / 20th Century. | JUVENILE FICTION / Social
Issues / Prejudice & Racism.
Classification: LCC PZ7.S6397 St 2016 (print) | LCC PZ7.S6397 (ebook) | DDC
[Fic]--dc23
LC record available at http://lccn.loc.gov/2015046700

For all the Indian children who attended such institutions

Acknowledgements

The author thanks Bard Young, Steve McDuff, Rod Clark, Chinua Achebe, James Welch, Ursula K. Le Guin, Howard Zinn, Norman Mailer, Joe Bruchac, Tony Hillerman, Roxanne Dunbar-Ortiz, Michael Dorris, Catherine Creger, Dan and Karol Lynn Johnson, and Amber Johnson for their insightful suggestions, as well as the numerous Indian elders from across America who shared their personal stories. To Winston Groom (Forrest Gump) who said this novel would give America a black eye and tried to convince me not to publish it: it's never a bad thing to tell the truth. The myth "How Raven Brought Light to the World" (Chapter 9) is from the author's The Raven and the Totem.

"Kill the Indian to Save the Man."
—Richard Henry Pratt, Headmaster
Carlisle Indian School, 1879

Contents

Four Indian children from very different parts of America, taken from their families, their lives immutably changed by an institution designed to eradicate their identity, to make them into something else—to make them less Indian. And no matter where they came from—north, south, east or west—their stories are representative of every story, every stolen life. So far from home, and without family to protect them, only their friendship would help them endure.

This story is a work of fiction.

Every word is true.

STEALING INDIANS

Chapter One

LUCY SECONDCHIEF could scarcely remember what her father looked like anymore. It had been four years since he died.

To a thirteen-year-old, four years is a long time.

As she set two spoons and two chipped bowls on a rickety table, Lucy remembered the day of her father's funeral and how people kept stopping by their little, tilted cabin on the frozen tundra, telling her mother how sad they were for her loss. Others stopped by the community center delivering food for the after-service supper. There were boxes of fry bread and biscuits, spaghetti noodles and canned spaghetti sauce, cardboard boxes of frozen moose meat and caribou meat, and two brown bags full of dried salmon strips. They brought coffee and tea, paper plates and bowls, napkins—everything necessary to feed an entire village.

The loss of her father was accompanied by more loss.

Some people, mostly old friends of her father's that Lucy hadn't seen in a long time, came to say how much money her father owed them. He must have owed a great deal because by the end of the day, Lucy's mother had given away all of her father's tools, two rifles, and a large stack of lumber, with which he had planned to expand the small, sagging cabin. One man was owed so much, so he said, that Lucy's mother let him take the entire sled-dog team that her husband had used to run his trap line. The man even took the sled.

Lucy spent the whole day sitting on a small chair beside the crackling wood stove, listening quietly to all the conversations that came and left the house each time the door opened or closed. She sat that way all day just listening and holding tight to the cheap, ragged doll her father had brought her nearly a year before when he came back from the city. It was her only toy. Her grandmother used to try to take it away from her during winter. She said that children weren't allowed to play with toys of any kind because if the winter knew that children were enjoying the slow winter months, it would stay around even longer.

On the night of her father's funeral, the sky was filled with northern lights. It was the most intense display anyone had ever seen. Lucy knew that the lights, the aurora, were a bad omen, a malevolent force that comes down to carry people away. Some stories say the lights are the spirits of the dead marching into the sky. Hunters in the wilderness brandished knives to keep them at bay. Parents told children to stay quiet on such nights, so the lights wouldn't hear them. Lucy had once seen some boys challenge the lights, standing nervously outside calling to the sky and whistling. But eventually they all ran back inside their cabins out of fear.

But on the night of her father's funeral, when the lights were at their very brightest, Lucy walked right out into the middle of a great field, stood beneath the shimmering stars and the dancing aurora, and yelled to the lights, demanding them to take her away. Her mother came out from the cabin, calling to her. The lights heard Lucy's defiance and dropped down from the star-raddled sky, encircling the young girl within shimmering red and green waves. The whole village watched in disbelief from behind frosted windows as the girl just stood there. Sled dogs belonging to other villagers, sitting atop their little straw-filled houses, began to bark and howl. Others cowered with their bushy tails tucked between their legs.

No one could remember anything like it.

24

Instead of running, little Lucy Secondchief just stood where she was, right in the middle of a great spruce-edged field, until she began to laugh. She laughed so loud that her echo returned all the way from the far, white mountains thirty miles distant across the wide, silty river.

After that, she never cried again for her dead father.

Her mother still wept every night, though, not so much from loneliness, not simply because she missed her husband, but because the life of a widow in a small village is a sad one.

Life was hard, but Lucy and her mother managed.

All through the intolerable winter, her mother worked a trap line every morning. She would get up early, drink a cup of weak tea made from the dry leaves of a local plant called Labrador tea, put on her parka, winter boots, gloves, and hat, and strike out into the wintered hills on snowshoes. In spite of the cold, Lucy's mother always paused at the top of the hill overlooking the little valley where her cabin sat just below the shadows cast by spruce trees, the sun barely reaching above their tops during this time of year, and waved to Lucy. She'd stay out there all morning, alone in the whiteness, checking rabbit snares and resetting them as needed. Sometimes she'd catch a martin or a weasel, which she would trade for the things she and Lucy needed. She'd go out even when the temperature was thirty degrees below zero. She had to. On a good day, she'd bring home at least one scrawny rabbit for their pot.

But most days were not good, and Lucy's mother would bring home only sadness and hunger in the empty rucksack. On those days, they would sit in the small, dark room that was their cabin, lit by a single, flickering candle, and sip hot broth made from boiled leftover bones from the day before.

In every measurable way, all they had was each other.

But Lucy and her mother had survived, were surviving. In the spring they set fish traps beneath small, swollen creeks to catch suckers and whitefish. In the summer they sometimes caught salmon stranded in the shallow gravel channels of the great river. In the fall they gathered berries. During the second winter after her husband died, Lucy's mother shot a cow moose that came close to the cabin. It was illegal to shoot a female moose like that, out of season and without a license, but their cabin was far enough away from the rest of the village that no one heard; no one came to investigate, and, fortunately, not the game warden. If he had caught them, he would have taken away the woman's rifle.

Although their bellies were empty and aching much of the time, their nights were filled with a kind of happiness, at least a contentment that comes of a sense of place, of belonging, of loving and being loved. Every night, Lucy's mother would fire up the small sauna behind the cabin, and the two would sit in the dark—sweating, talking, singing, telling stories, gently lashing each other with swatches of spruce, the scent of the boughs permeating the close room. When Lucy and her mother became too hot, they would step out into the cold night air and rub handfuls of snow on their naked, brown skin to cool down. After the sauna, they would sit inside the warm cabin—their tiny wood stove rattling—combing and braiding each other's long, black hair. Her mother's hair had long strands of gray, even though she was not yet forty. Before bed, they told traditional stories about Raven, drank weak tea, and prayed for more rabbits.

One night, toward the end of the short-lived fall, after most leaves had fallen and bears began to search for winter dens, as mother and daughter lay in bed while the moon lay on the edge of the windowsill, Lucy told of a dream she remembered from a few nights earlier.

"I dreamt that I was in a strange house and there was a table full of food. There were all kinds of breads and meats and cheese," she whispered, her eyes open and staring at the ceiling. "There was even a basket full of apples."

"It sounds like a good dream," her mother whispered through the darkness.

Lucy was quiet for a long time before she spoke again.

"There was all this food, enough for many people. Then I saw you outside, and I tried to let you in, but the doors and windows would not open. You were alone and starving, your eyes were dark and hollow, and your hair was white. I yelled to you, but you did not answer. I tried to break the glass with a chair, but it would not break. Then you walked away. I screamed for you to come back, but you did not hear me. When you were too far away to see, I turned around and there were other Indian children sitting at the table eating all the food. But then they didn't look like Indians any more. I stood by the door crying until there was nothing left for me."

The tired woman turned toward her daughter, raised herself on one elbow, and kissed her on the forehead.

"It was only a dream, child," she said as she rolled back into the warm spot her body had made in the thin mattress and pulled the heavy blankets up to her chin.

The next day, Lucy was outside carrying a stack of firewood when a big, tall-roofed black car pulled into the drive. It was a cold and windy day, even for fall. Lucy's mother came out from inside the house, wearing the tattered, old shawl she wore when she was inside the house.

Two men stepped from the car and walked up to Lucy's mother. From where she stood, Lucy could see the taller man pull a piece of paper from a black briefcase and hand it to her. Her mother looked at the paper for a long moment, but she could not read it. She had never learned to read. Nevertheless, she knew what the document said. Every Indian parent knew what it said. All across the country, Indian families were given the same piece of paper, which proclaimed the end to families. The paper was the law. It was the government's authority to steal Indian children from their families and send them far from their homes and villages.

The law was for the sake of the children, a ticket to a better life free from the burdens of poverty and ignorance. The paper was the law that sent them to Kansas, Oregon, the Dakotas, California, Oklahoma, and Pennsylvania—anywhere far enough away so that they would forget what it means to be Indian.

"It's in the child's best interest," the government men told the distraught and grieving families.

The men walked toward Lucy, still standing with her two arms full of firewood. When they were close, she dropped the pile and tried to run to her mother. But they grabbed her and dragged her to the car, pushed her into the back seat, and closed the door. There were no handles on the inside.

Lucy was trapped.

She screamed and kicked. Then the low, powerful engine started again, and the car slowly turned around. Lucy stood on the back seat with her feet pressed into the cushions and looked out the slender back window as the car drove down the long, rutted driveway. She cried out for her mother and beat her bound fists against the curve of the thick glass.

Just then a great wind arose, shaking the last orange and yellow and brown leaves from trees, raking them up from the ground, the brittle and rotting leaves swirling and twisting across the rutted driveway. It began to sleet, angry and lashing. A large branch broke off from a tree and fell across the road ahead, almost blocking the car.

Lucy watched through tears as her mother ran behind the black car, her tattered shawl flapping in the wind like a ragged bird, saw her slip and fall in the muddy ruts, her thin, brown arms reaching out as she cried for her daughter.

SIMON LONE FIGHT was running across an arid desert, dodging rattlesnakes and scorpions, jumping over tumbleweeds spinning across the red earth.

Simon was always running.

He ran to and from everything—from the grocery store to the service station where his uncle worked, from his ramshackle home to the community hall where everyone played bingo on Fridays and Saturday nights, from the future and toward the past. He ran all day across his reservation, which was so destitute that even the few small streams winding across the arid landscape were almost always empty-pocketed and bone-dry.

Simon ran across the hot, red desert, through its echoing canyons and arroyos, over buttes and mesas, jumping over boulders and tumbleweeds, startling jackrabbits and lizards, his long black hair shining in the sun.

No one on his reservation could keep up with him.

Even his shadow had to stop to rest, bent double under a high sun, winded, gray shadow-sweat dripping on the thirsty earth. No one had ever seen anything like him. He'd run up and down the highway, waving at cars and smiling the whole time. His mother used to joke that Simon went straight from crawling to running—just grabbed his milk bottle one day and took off running out the front door, his little, chubby baby legs carrying him all the way to the edge of the reservation before his father caught up with him in a pickup truck.

And he'd been running ever since.

Simon's parents died on his thirteenth birthday. Both of them, father and mother, in a car crash going around Dead Man's Bend coming home from a funeral. When a drunk driver swerves toward you on a narrow turn with a two hundred forty foot drop, there's no place to go, no place to run or hide, no safe space in all the world.

After his parents' funeral, Simon returned to his mobile home resting on cement blocks, changed out of his secondhand black suit and tie, which he had borrowed from his cousin who was several inches taller and more than a dozen pounds heavier, drank a glass of cold water in one long, breathless series of gulps, ate a bologna-and-cheese sandwich with pickles and sliced green tomatoes, and went out for a run.

He was gone for three days.

No one knew what had happened to Simon. The whole reservation heard about his disappearance. Men and women, boys and girls from all over went out looking for him. Twenty-seven pickups—all with mismatched tires and expired license plates—left the parking lot at Fat Mabel's Bar & Grill, each driver assigned a specific area to search. The congregation of the First Baptist Church of Indian Conversion cooked up a giant batch of fry bread to feed all the searchers. The police put out an all-points bulletin. Fliers were printed and circulated all over the reservation, stapled to utility poles, to storefronts, and duct-taped to abandoned trucks and empty fuel barrels rusting in fields. Someone even stapled signs at all five holes of Big Red Chief's Mini-Golf.

Even Simon's dog, Tonto, went out looking for him. They named the dog that because he followed the boy everywhere, like a faithful sidekick who couldn't speak a word of English.

Luckily, his second cousin on his father's side, Norman Fury, found him running along a backcountry road five towns over. He saw Simon at first from a distance, bouncing slightly with each jogging stride, saw him through heat waves writhing up from the melting, black asphalt, like an apparition only partly of this world.

The boy almost made it to the state line.

During the next year, Simon was passed from relative to relative, from one cramped house of poverty to another. No one even knew that his fourteenth birthday had come and gone. In all of his many moves he never once had a room of his own. Each time he moved, Tonto went with him. They were inseparable.

One day, Tonto, looking down the one lane dirt road, began to bark at a growing black dot on the burning horizon, a cloud of dust building behind it. Simon didn't know why he felt suddenly afraid of the black dot. He crept behind a corner of the house and watched as the approaching dot turned into a car. When it turned down their driveway, Simon and his dog scooted off, staying low and hiding behind the leaning outhouse—both trying not to breathe as they watched. From his crouching position, the boy saw two white men in dark suits with dark briefcases step out of the black, high-roofed automobile. His grandparents came out from their house to speak to the men. Simon couldn't hear a word they said, but it was clear that his grandfather was arguing with the men. After a while, his grandfather sat down on a small stool and dropped his head low, while his grandmother went inside the house, calling for Simon.

When she came out alone, the men went inside to search the house. By the time they started checking the yard and the outhouse, Simon was already a mile back in the canyons, running faster than he had ever run before, the panic swirling inside him, pushing him along like a hard wind.

The men came for him three more times that month, but Simon was always gone before they even turned off the heavy engine inside the chest of the big, black car.

One day at the end of summer, his grandparents told him they were going into town to sell hay. They asked Simon to come along, promising him ice cream if he helped unload the heavy bales. The cramped cab of the old truck allowed for only two, so Simon and Tonto jumped into the back and sat atop of the small cluster of bales. They loved riding in the open bed, the cooling rush of wind pouring over them as the truck sped down the road, jack rabbits jumping from the gravel shoulders.

Dark clouds were building on the horizon. A storm was approaching. Simon was worried that it would rain before they returned home.

But before they arrived in town, the truck turned on a road leading to a small train station at the edge of town, more whistle stop than station. Simon recognized the place. It was where ranchers sold their livestock for immediate loading on freight trains. His grandfather shut off the engine, climbed out from the cab, and closed the creaking door. His grandmother waited inside.

"Come on down from there, boy," he said, lowering the tailgate.

Simon and Tonto jumped down from the bed, kicking up dust as they landed.

"You gonna load these bales on the train, Grandpa?" Simon asked, confused because he had never known the old man to sell hay to anyone but locals. Besides, the dozen bales on the truck hardly made up a load worth shipping on a train.

His grandfather didn't answer but looked at his pocket watch instead.

"Five minutes," he said, as he slid the watch back into his pocket.

While they waited, Simon tossed sticks for Tonto to fetch. They were out in the nearby fields playing when the train whistled its arrival. Simon ran back, ready to help his grandfather. The locomotive engine was so loud that the boy didn't hear the high-roofed black car pulling up next to the old truck. Two men slid out like snakes and grabbed the boy from behind.

Simon struggled to break away, screaming. His dog barked and bit the leg of one of the men. His grandmother covered her eyes with her hands and wept inside the cab, the sun scorched the parched landscape, a lizard darted beneath a rock, and his grandfather stood by sullenly watching the whole thing, squeezing and squeezing his empty hands inside his empty pockets.

"You got to go with these men," he said, his voice filled with sadness.

"But I want to stay with you!" Simon cried, still trying to free himself.

The old man swallowed his love for his grandson, swallowed his love of his own dead son, and swallowed a thousand years of pride.

"You must go to school," he said. "It's the law."

The sound of those words made Simon hate the school already, whatever it was, wherever it was.

On an imitation leather seat aboard the train's passenger car, the young Indian boy who loved to run, who could outrun everything but this moment, looked out the window as the train started to move. The powerful engine picked up speed, and Simon watched as the only world he had ever known began to slide away: the mesas, the dull-pink earth beneath the vaulted sky, the arroyos and canyons, the thirsty fields, the hogans, and the government housing that all looked the same.

Simon watched his faithful dog running beside the train, barking at it as if he might turn the great machine around, just as he sometimes did wayward sheep. Simon watched him struggling to keep pace, until he could run no longer and slowed to a trot and then stopped altogether and sat in the middle of the tracks and howled.

For many rattling miles, Simon Lone Fight stared out the smudged glass, quietly crying, his heart bursting, his small brown hands pressed sadly against the latched window, closed tight as a fist.

NOAH BOYSCOUT was hunting alone on a thinly veiled snowy landscape, the waggling trees covered in rime. He pulled his fur-trimmed parka hood from his head, looked far ahead, his eyes narrowed.

He could see his breath as he breathed.

Noah stood quietly on the trail, watching the tree line and listening for something that did not come. He thought he had seen movement from the corner of his eye—sudden and fleeting. The day was cold and bright, the sky deep blue, the distant mountains glowing almost pink in the angled light of midwinter. There was only a slight breeze. A squirrel scampered about the top of a nearby spruce tree, deftly tossing tiny cones to the ground, stopping occasionally to make certain the boy was not stealing his food. After a while, the boy adjusted the rucksack on his back and slung the rifle over his shoulder, raised his parka hood, and resumed his homeward trek.

The sound of brittle snow beneath his feet measured the white miles.

Halfway to his family's cabin in the valley far below, Noah again thought he saw something moving, a flashing among the trees, only for a second. He stopped and squinted hard, taking in every little thing—the almost imperceptible sway of treetops, a small flock of tiny birds alighting on a willow, a raven in the distance flying into the low sun. Although he saw nothing that concerned him, the young Indian removed a glove, reached into a pocket on the front of his parka, and pulled out what few bullets remained.

There were only three.

He had used the rest to shoot the half dozen rabbits that filled his old canvas pack. After rolling the small brass cartridges across his palm, he slid them back into the deep pocket.

Noah had hunted in these hills for much of his young life. Although only fourteen, he was already learning the laws of the untamed land. He knew the trails that wound from the valley into the hills and, further still, toward the mountains. Grizzly country. Occasionally, small bands of caribou migrated into the hills, milling about all winter in search of food and escape from deep snow and hungry wolves. In all his years, Noah had never seen a wolf, but he had, from time to time, come across their tracks. Once, he even stumbled on a wolf kill. Little remained of the animal—a young caribou, mostly hair, the head with its glazed-over eyes still open, some bones—at the center of the red paw-trampled snow all around the clearing.

Noah pulled the thick glove over his hand and took a hard look across the wintered forest before continuing his shuffling descent from the hills, one hand gripping the swaying leather sling of his rifle. He loved the vastness of the land, its power, its great silence and beauty. He loved the time he spent on it, the deep quiet of thinking and daydreaming. Here, among the spindly spruce trees, the wind and flitting birds, he was himself. He was home. He did not belong in the world of man. Nature is harsh—even brutal—but she is honest. A person knows where he stands. Though still a boy, Noah knew these things, and the truth made him happy and sad all at once. As a half-breed—only partially Indian—he was already an outcast of sorts, not fully fitting in anywhere. Other people, his own parents and friends included, did not understand him. They did not understand his need for the wild or why he sat for hours sometimes, listening to ravens or the sounds of wind and river.

Noah found peace where others found nothing.

More than anyone else, his own mother did not understand him. She was not Indian, and she did not understand things the way Indians do. Sometimes, Noah would come home from a day alone in the forest all excited about an experience.

"Mother!" he once yelled, as he entered the small cabin and closed the door.

"What is it, Noah?" she asked, putting down the dish she was washing, knowing that her young son would ramble on about something in which she had no interest or, worse, that he would tell another of his tales about taking chances in the wilderness.

While taking off his parka and boots, the boy happily related his story.

"I was sitting by my campfire eating my lunch, when a fox came and stood close, maybe a dozen steps away. I started speaking to him real soft, asking him to stay and visit. When he came closer, I could see he was nervous, but I kept speaking soft and smiling at him. When he was only a couple steps away, I held out my hand and he came up to it and smelled my palm!"

As she listened, his mother's boredom turned to concern. Her white face showed more and more a grim intensity as she listened.

The boy continued his incredible story.

"Then I slowly raised my hand and stroked the fur on his head, rubbing behind his ears. He didn't seem to mind. I think he liked it, so I started petting his head with both hands. Then he came in even closer and pressed his body against mine. I wrapped my arms around him and held him close, petting his back and belly while whispering to him, telling him what a pretty fox he was."

His mother's expression now was of troubled worry tinged with anger.

"After a while he just pulled away and trotted back into the forest. You should have seen him, Mom. He was such a nice fox. I think we're friends now. Maybe I'll shoot a rabbit for him next time I see him."

That wasn't the only time Noah had told of such encounters. In fact, nearly every week or so he had another story to tell, like the time a newborn moose calf teetered clumsily out of a willow patch, walked right up to him, pressed its head against his hip, curled up on the ground beside him and took a nap with its little blonde moose head snuggled on the boy's lap. They sat like that for hours, the boy gently caressing the top of the calf's head and its long, stiff mane, the moose sleeping, warmed by the high summer sun.

Of course, the boy kept a wary eye out for the mother.

After such stories his mother would kneel down before her young son, grab him by the shoulders, and tell him to stay away from those dirty animals, saying how they might bite him, how they might have rabies. To his mother, the idea of humans and animals dwelling on the same land, that their lives are intertwined, related, that they are somehow brothers and sisters was an idea that was at best troubling and at worst disgusting, even horrible. To her, the land was fraught only with menace.

Noah adjusted the biting leather rifle sling as he continued his lonely descent from the snow-clad hills. A raven flying overhead landed on a tree branch and watched the shuffling figure. As the figure drew close, the bird cawed out to the boy, who cawed back. Noah spoke raven and grouse. Pleased with the news, the raven flew away, its sharp eyes searching the earth for something to eat.

A half hour later, Noah saw them clearly for the first time, hiding behind trees and deadfalls on either side of the trail. From where he stood he counted six or seven, but there may have been more. They were still far away, watching him and turning to look at one another, waiting for a signal. They were gray-coated, and they easily vanished in the gray-white landscape.

The boy knew they had been following him for a long time. He had sensed them earlier up in the hills. He increased his pace, looking left and right of the trail at all times. The wolves were working their way closer. They knew they had lost the element of surprise, but they had sheer numbers in their favor.

Seven of them against one skinny boy.

Within minutes they were close enough that Noah could hear the sound of panting. He stopped, slid the rifle from his shoulder with one hand and the pack from his back with the other. With the rucksack on the ground beside him, he worked the bolt of his single-shot rifle—a boy's rifle—and reached into the pocket for the extra shells. He was afraid, but he would stand his ground.

For an instant, and only for an instant, Noah wondered in that way men sometimes wonder about the absurdity of their circumstances. At a time when many homes had a television, when the energy of the atom had been harnessed, when a beeping man-made satellite actually raced across the night sky, here was a boy standing in a far white field in the middle of nowhere, facing a pack of encircling wolves—snarling and baring and snapping their teeth.

Knowing it unlikely that he could kill a wolf with his small rifle, Noah fired one shot into the air to scare them away. But the sound of a .22 in vast and open country is hardly enough to frighten even a small bird. The wolves stopped for a moment, their ears perked, their shaggy heads cocked sideways, but their response was curiosity, not fear. They resumed their methodical attack almost immediately. They moved nervously around the boy who turned to meet them, loading another round into the breech. He couldn't spare another warning bullet; each one would have to count.

Then two of the wolves, pack leaders, stopped and held their heads high to smell the crisp winter air, their noses black and wet. Noah had noticed others of the pack doing the same, at some distance, but this time—the seven wolves close enough so that Noah had to turn his head from side to side to see all of them—the behavior caught his eye. Every wolf was sniffing the air. A realization then flashed in Noah's mind.

The wolves weren't after him. They smelled the rabbits. They wanted the rabbits.

Slowly, his eyes fixed on the wolves. He stooped and felt for the top of the canvas pack. With one hand he loosened the thick strings, which cinched it closed, and pulled out a dead, stiff rabbit. It was like a slow-motion magic trick. The wolves stopped their sniffing. Now their eyes, yellow and keen, proved what their noses had told them. This was what they wanted. It was what they had wanted all along. Noah stood up and with all his might tossed the rigid rabbit beyond their heads. They turned and ran after it. One after another, he flung all the dead rabbits as far as he could, and one after another the wolves broke off, each finding its own easy meal. While they were busy, Noah grabbed the empty bag and started for home, frequently looking over his shoulder, his nearly useless rifle at the ready.

Bend after bend, only his lean shadow followed him down the frozen trail, as the winter sun sank lower, barely skimming the bulging edge of the world.

Night had shredded and gulped the land as voraciously as the wolves their rabbits when Noah finally arrived at his small cabin. Light from inside shone through the darkness, and, as if struck from flint, sparks slipped up through the chimney pipe from the wood stove and danced skyward, taking their place among the stars. Noah paused to watch rising sparks before noticing a tall black car parked in the driveway. He had not seen it at first. Thinking only that his parents had strange visitors, Noah knelt to remove his snowshoes. Once removed, he leaned them upright against the porch, stepped into the warm house, closed and latched the heavy door, and hung his parka on a nail near the wood stove.

His parents sat at a small table drinking tea with a white man Noah had not seen before. As the stranger in a black business suit and hat, which he did not remove, stood to greet him, his mother began to cry and ran into the bedroom, slamming the door. Noah's father comforted and assured his son that his mother would be all right, then motioned for him to sit beside him. The man with the briefcase placed several folders on the wobbly table and spoke about how Noah had to go away to a school just for Indian boys and girls. He opened one of the folders and spread out several pictures of the school. One photograph showed a group of unsmiling Indian children standing beneath an iron archway with the school's name spelled out in black letters. Numerous buildings and a neatly rowed cemetery were barely visible in the background.

While stars slid slowly across the world's cold rim, the man who had arrived in the car as black as the night sat across the small, paper-strewn table calmly telling the boy how he was to be sent there without his family, how he would benefit from the marvelous opportunity granted him by the government, how he would make his family and his village proud.

ELIJAH HIGH HORSE fired two shots across the narrow lake. It was a hundred yards to the other side, more or less. The shots roared in the cup of the frosted valley, and a flock of small birds lifted from a leafless tree and flew over the white hill.

Elijah lowered his rifle and rubbed his shoulder after the jolts from the big rifle's recoil. His first cousin, Johnny Big Jim, stood beside him, looking across the lake, his long, black hair lifting slightly in the breeze.

"What are you shooting at?" he asked, squinting to see the distant shore.

"That deer on the sand bar. Right there," Elijah replied, pointing.

Johnny's eyes followed his cousin's arm and pointing finger.

"I don't see anything," he said, still squinting. "There's nothing there."

But Elijah worked the bolt, shoving another cartridge into the chamber. He brought the butt of the rifle to his shoulder, set it tight, aimed carefully, and fired again.

Johnny raised his own beat-up rifle and looked through its scope across the water.

"What are you shooting at?" he asked again, his voice growing impatient.

"That big buck standing right there. Can't you see it? Look at the size of those antlers!" he exclaimed, his head moving slightly left as if he were following something moving on the other side.

"Damn it. There he goes. Damn. He got away."

Johnny raised his rifle once more, looked for a moment, and then turned to his cousin.

"There wasn't nothing there," he said, shaking his head. The tone of his voice was perplexed, but honest. He wasn't kidding.

"It was right there, standing on the shore by those willows. You had to see it!"

The cousins, their mothers being sisters, had grown up together. Everyone in the village grew up together in one way or another. It was too small not to be otherwise. Although barely fourteen, he boys spent a great deal of time in the forest hunting and fishing. They loved the woods, the wildness of it. When they went into the woods, they thought of themselves as hunters, the way hunters were meant to be. They were Indians. This is what they were sure they knew. For the cousins, who were as irreverent as any 14-year-olds, their time in the woods was nearly sacred—a time to be what their grandfathers had been long ago. For Elijah and Johnny, the woods was not a place for joking.

They stood arguing as the sun set over the hill and its shadow fell into the valley. It would be dark soon.

"I'm not joking, Elijah!" Johnny said for the fifth or sixth time. "There was nothing there. You were shooting at nothing."

But his cousin stood his ground, certain of what he had seen.

Finally, near darkness, they overturned a canoe, which had been left partially hidden among trees for hunters to use, and paddled across the lake to where Elijah had seen the deer and walked up and down the shoreline for a while before giving up for the night.

"I don't get it," Elijah finally said, puzzled, his warm breath rising on the air like the flock of small white birds they had seen earlier. "It was right here. I swear."

They both looked down again. The ground was sandy and so soft that they could see their own boot tracks weaving around where they had searched for sign. But there were no other tracks of any kind. Nothing had walked across that spot in days or maybe weeks. There had been no deer—only emptiness and the rolling hills of spruce and pine in the distance.

As darkness settled upon the land, curling on itself like a fox trying to get comfortable for the long night, the two young Indians paddled back across the flat, dark water. A loon called from the far side, and an owl's hoot came softly through the night.

That night, their campfire embers glowing outside, they lay inside their fluttering tent talking about the vanishing buck.

"I saw it as clearly as I see you right now," Elijah whispered. "I'm serious. I had it dead on."

Once he fell asleep, Elijah slept restlessly, dreaming strange dreams. He awoke often, thinking he heard rustlings outside the tent. A bear or cougar perhaps. Two years earlier, a hungry cougar had come down from the hills and killed his family's dog. *But maybe this is nothing,* he thought after listening for a long time, warm in his sleeping bag.

It was a long night.

The next morning they packed up camp and hiked home. They stopped at their grandfather's house. He was a traditional chief and a deeply spiritual person. He had been born back when Indians still spoke their inherited language, when they remembered the old ways, before things changed forever. He had told them the old stories. The old man was outside, wearing a baseball cap, blue jeans and a thick red flannel shirt with suspenders. He was changing a tire on his car. The boys helped.

"Grandfather," Elijah said after the tire was mounted and the lug nuts tightened. "I have to tell you something."

He told the story of the previous evening, how he had seen the big buck and shot at it, twice. Johnny told the part how they searched for but found no tracks in the soft earth.

"It was like the buck was never there at all," Elijah said.

The old man sat down stiffly on a rusty fifty-five-gallon drum turned on its side. There were dozens of them scattered around the field like wild flowers. At the far edge of the field near the tree line, abandoned cars, two Chevrolets and a Desoto, decayed slowly, becoming homes for small animals.

His grandfather listened without interrupting, his eyes focused on the woods beyond the field. Then he looked at his grandson for a long time before he spoke.

"That's because it wasn't really there, Elijah," he said slowly, the way elders always spoke, as if nothing was in a hurry any-more—not their thoughts, not their words.

"You saw the spirit of a deer, its ghost. When an animal dies—a fox, beaver, grizzly bear, coyote, or deer—its spirit stays in this world. This is heaven to them. They still walk around doing the same things they always did. They don't know they're dead. But people can't see them. They exist only in the spirit world. They are all around us, even now, here in this field, in those cedars and spruce on the hillside. Even the spirits of salmon swim the rivers following their children and grandchildren as they spawn each summer, and dense, reeling flocks of invisible birds blot out the sun. Only a shaman can see them."

Elijah knelt down closer to his grandfather as the old chief continued.

"When you were born, we knew that you would be a shaman one day. When the local priest came to baptize you, your nose started bleeding when the holy water touched you. All the elders remember that day. But no one can tell when it will begin. Some-times it doesn't happen until one is very old and is willing to see the world of the dead. Sometimes it happens too soon, when one is unwilling to believe his eyes. The visions can use up a weak man, overwhelm him. Not every man can carry the gift. We knew that you would see what you must see when it was time. There was no reason to tell you while you were so young. We knew that one day you would come to us."

Elijah and Johnny walked the old chief to his house, helped

carry in two five-gallon jugs of drinking water, which they placed in a corner near the wood stove and left. Then the two boys walked down to an open area along the river, which was low. This late in the fall, rivers began to shrink before the long winter freeze. They built a fire and rolled two big, round firewood logs close to sit on. They didn't talk for a long time but stared into the fire and out across the river toward the great mountains in the distance.

Elijah finally broke the silence.

"I have to tell you something," he said quietly.

Johnny turned away from the spell of the fire to face his cousin.

"That deer wasn't the first time. Last winter, I was hunting rabbit up in the hills behind my father's winter cabin. It had been snowing hard for a long time and the snow was deep. I got up one morning and snow-shoed up into the hills. I must have shot five or six rabbits, I think. I don't really remember."

Johnny turned his body more toward his cousin, and waited.

"On the way back, I saw a buffalo. It was all white. I had never seen anything like it. The snow was so deep that it had a hard time moving. I don't know why, but I started chasing it. I wasn't going to shoot it or nothing. I was just having fun. I remember it as clearly as I see you sitting here. It was running, stumbling in the deep, crusted snow. I can still see it in my mind—its breath rising up, its eyes wide and white in fear. I could even see its muscles moving under its white hide. I kept chasing it, laughing and out of breath. Little by little, it got farther away until it finally reached the timberline and vanished. I stood in the deep field catching my breath, listening to the wind and the silence. I took off my hat and gloves to cool down."

Johnny looked at his cousin, who had turned back toward the fire, a tear rolling down his face. He didn't understand why Elijah should be crying.

"I remember I turned around and started back for the cabin

when it dawned on me that there was something wrong. I realized there were only *my* tracks in the snow. I walked all around looking for that buffalo's tracks. I walked nearly to the tree line where it disappeared. I looked for so long that the sun went away, and I was left alone in the dark. I never found a single track, only mine. I didn't know what to make of it."

Elijah was silent after that, trying to reposition a log in the fire with a long stick. When he was satisfied, he spoke again.

"I've never told anyone about it until now."

Johnny nodded without saying anything.

As the low, red sun set over the far mountains, and darkness settled over the land as soft as falling snow while casting long shadows in the quiet forest, the two young Indians sat beside the dying embers of a fire as stars began to shine and as the indifferent spirits of animals began to walk around them, beside them, through them—while the cold night began to sleep.

A week later, just before the first snow, below a long wedge of migrating geese, Elijah's father drove him to the train station, handed him a tight-packed suitcase, a brown paper bag filled with two large pieces of fried chicken and a peanut-butter-and-jelly sandwich, two apples, and a one-way ticket.

Johnny was there to say goodbye. He wasn't going. The government had already taken two of his older brothers and a sister. He was allowed to stay. Not all Indian children were taken from their homes. That would have been unnecessary and, practically speaking, impossible. Neither the available room nor the funding would allow it. The government's goal could be achieved by taking only some, similar to the way the government didn't draft every young man from large families into military service during the war against the Nazis and the Japanese, over for only a few years.

"Be careful," Johnny whispered as he held his best friend close. "Watch yourself."

Johnny had heard stories from his older brothers and sister. He knew about the schools, about what happened in them, the sadness, the despair, things better left unspoken. With that said, he straddled his bike, waved one last time, and pedaled homeward.

When the porter blew his shiny whistle announcing the train's impending departure, Elijah's father left without saying goodbye, shuffling toward their old truck without once looking back, his eyes on the ground the entire time, as if he were looking for the pocketful of pride he had lost somewhere a long time ago.

Frightened and alone, Elijah High Horse slung his knapsack across a shoulder, lifted the suitcase with the other hand, and stepped aboard the passenger compartment as the whole line of cars jolted forward. The young Indian found a seat beside a window and sat for a long time quietly staring at the small piece of paper with the name of a place he had never heard of. He cried on and off during the next two hundred miles, wiping away tears with quick, frequent, but discreet motions so that the man sitting across from him never noticed.

Chapter Two

AFTER HOURS of driving the narrow, winding highway, the high-roofed black car with little Lucy Secondchief sleeping on the back seat stopped at a small diner. The sound of a door opening awakened her. Lucy watched as the taller man rose out from the passenger seat and went inside. The driver, shorter and heavier than the other, sat behind the steering wheel smoking cigarettes, one after the other, his window rolled half way down to let out the billowing cloud. After what seemed a long time, the other man came out of the diner with a bag in his hand.

"I got everything," he said, in a dull monotone to the driver as he sat down and closed the heavy, squeaking door.

The car started again, turned out of the gravel parking lot, and accelerated back onto the highway. The tall man pulled a burger wrapped in tin foil from the brown paper bag and handed it to the driver. Then he pulled one out for himself. He unwrapped a corner of the tinfoil and took a bite.

"What about the kid?" the driver asked, looking back at Lucy through the rearview mirror.

"I didn't get her nothing."

"What do you mean you didn't get her anything?"

"I didn't even think about it, that's all," replied the man holding the paper bag on his lap. He took another bite and chewed with his mouth open.

The driver looked at the mirror again. He could barely see the little girl's face and was impressed by the haunting look he saw there. Even in the dimming light, he could make out an odd expression, perhaps a kind of sadness, perhaps a sadness so deep that light barely reflected from her face, as if her great sadness were some kind of black hole from which nothing could escape. He didn't like how the look made him feel.

He didn't like the little girl. It wouldn't matter if he did. She was a job to him, a delivery, that's all. He was sick and tired of transporting Indian children. He turned his eyes away from the mirror, concentrating on the road in an effort to lose his awareness of the despair seated so close behind him.

"Even Indians gotta eat! Give her my damn fries!" the driver barked at the other man, his voice angry.

The tall man sighed impatiently, turned around in his seat, and handed Lucy a small, grease-soaked bag.

Lucy had never tasted French fries before. She liked the saltiness.

After eating, she curled up on the back seat and slept, dreaming of her home and her mother as the shiny black car sped into the night toward a distant, unfamiliar future—sadness trailing in its wake like swirling black snow.

Several hours later, Lucy awoke to a gentle shaking.

"Wake up," the driver said, leaning over her, the back door open.

Lucy sat up and looked around. It was night. They were in another town, and street lights lit a corridor of darkness. Buildings surrounded her. Lights were on in some of the windows, but most were black. Nothing moved on the quiet street except a stray dog that crossed two blocks down.

"It's time to go. Get out of the car," ordered the man, stepping back to make room for her.

Lucy hopped down from the seat, rubbing her eyes and yawning. She was tired. She needed to pee.

"This is a bus station," the man said. "You're taking a bus for the rest of your trip."

He led her inside and told her to sit and wait in a hard, plastic chair, while he went to the counter and bought a one-way ticket.

Lucy wrinkled her nose. The station smelled stale. A few other people sat sleeping on the uncomfortable seats, each with a suitcase or cloth bag alongside. But Lucy had nothing, only the clothes she had been wearing when the men took her away. They were secondhand. Her blouse showed a repaired tear, where her mother had sewed one night while they sat in their warm cabin telling stories and drinking weak tea. Lucy reached for the torn place, felt the uneven stitches, felt her mother's rough fingers. Tears built in the corners of her eyes until they were too heavy and slid down her brown cheeks. A man sleeping nearby coughed, turned his head, muttered something, and fell back asleep. Lucy wiped away the tears with her sleeves until the cuffs were damp.

The driver returned. He knelt down and spoke gently.

"This is a ticket," he said, handing her the thick, pink paper. "A bus is going to take you the rest of the way. You have to go by yourself from here on. The bus driver will tell you when to get off. He'll be watching after you. Do you understand?" he asked, his voice softer and kinder than it had been before.

Lucy nodded as she rubbed the red welts on her wrists.

The man walked over to a vending machine between the men's and women's bathrooms, slid some coins into the slot and pulled hard on a lever until there was a clunking sound. He walked back to Lucy, handed her a candy bar, and told her to keep it in her pocket until later.

"It'll be a long ride," he said, careful not to look into the deep well of her eyes. "The driver knows where you're going. You'll have to do exactly as you are told, otherwise you could get in trouble. And you'll be in real trouble if you get off the bus when you're not supposed to."

Lucy nodded again. She didn't want to get into trouble.

"I need to pee," she said with her knees pressed together.

"Over there," the man nodded. The Ladies Room."

When she returned, the man who had taken her from her mother—from the only world she had ever known—sat in the hard, red, plastic seat beside her, without saying a further word, until it was time to board the bus.

When it came late in the night and opened its door for boarding. Lucy stepped up the tall stairs and walked down the dark, narrow aisle. Almost everyone on the bus was asleep. She found an empty seat near the back of the bus. She sat next to the window and looked around her. A man with skin as black as the night beyond the windowpane was sitting across from her. He was sleeping with his head against the window, his jacket wadded up for a pillow. Lucy had never seen a black person before. She stared at him for a long time until her head fell on her chest and she slid into a restless, uncomfortable sleep.

The bus was cold, and the little girl who had no jacket dreamed of falling snow, of frozen lakes and faraway hills, shivering as the rocking bus passed through the night, whispering or coughing through her fitful dreams, crossing an unfamiliar and ever-changing landscape, and an ever-expanding universe beneath a half-withered moon casting little light in the hopeless dark. Occasionally, she would wake up, glance drowsily out the window at the fleeting houses, dark against the sullen night, before falling asleep again, her head nodding or rolling back and forth with every bump and turn of the long and lengthening road.

The next morning the bus stopped at a bus depot that doubled as a service station in a small town that looked like all the other small towns it had passed through in the night.

"Ten minute break!" the driver yelled as he pulled a lever that opened the outward swinging door and stepped off the bus to light a cigarette.

Lucy had to go to the bathroom again. She stepped from the bus and asked the driver for directions.

"Over there," he said without looking, only pointing. "Don't forget," he continued. "Ten minutes."

Rushing back to the bus for fear of being left behind, Lucy found her seat occupied by an elderly white couple, the nearly bald man looking out the window, his wife reading a magazine. Lucy stood for several moments, not knowing what to do.

"What is it? What do you want?" the woman asked, looking up from her magazine, her expression signaling both confusion and irritation.

Lucy shuffled further toward the back and sat in the only remaining seat, on the aisle and next to a man who looked out of place in a blue suit and starched collar. He sat hunched over a thick book of church-choir music, making notes on a lined sheet of paper. He looked very fit for his age, she thought. One of the names on the tag on his leather briefcase read "Bard." She couldn't make out the last name. When she looked around, she saw an Indian boy sitting across the aisle from her beside a portly woman who was snoring. He looked to be about a year or two older, thirteen or fourteen. It was hard to tell. Lucy was small for her age, scrawny as a starved rabbit. The boy was wearing a dark blue shirt and blue jeans, the cuffs rolled up a couple of turns. His jacket was neatly folded on his lap beneath a brown grocery bag. As the bus driver boarded and closed the door, the boy leaned forward to speak.

"My name is Noah, Noah Boyscout," he said, smiling, holding out a green apple. "Want one?"

Lucy was hungry. Recalling that she had not yet eaten the candy bar the government man had given her, she took the apple, bit into it, and when she had finished chewing and swallowing half the apple, she replied.

"My name is Lucy," she said, smiling, her long, black hair strewn across her face.

The two young Indians sitting across from each other talked as the bus cruised across the next several hundred miles. Sometimes they took fitful naps. As the bus made its way south, small towns sprang up more and more often from the flattening earth. While an increasingly unfamiliar world passed by the closed windows throughout the day, Lucy and Noah talked about their homes and their families. They talked about the place where they were going, wondered to each other where it was, what it was like, what would become of them. When the elderly couple who had occupied Lucy's seat got off in some town, they took the vacant seats so they could sit together.

That evening the bus stopped in another small town. After so many, they all looked the same. Only the names changed.

Rising out of his seat, the bus driver walked toward the back of the bus and spoke to the two children.

"You gotta change buses here," he said. "Go to the counter and show them your tickets. They'll tell you which one, but this one ain't going that-away no more."

Lucy and Noah stepped down from the bus. The sun was going down. Tall grain bins speared up through the fat horizon. It would be dark in an hour or so. The man at the counter said their bus would not arrive for another hour. He told the two children to sit and wait in the drab terminal until they heard their bus announced. But the Indians were tired of sitting. They wanted to stretch their legs. As they walked down the long street lined with storefronts, which were already closed for the day, Noah memorized street signs and store names so they wouldn't get lost.

They were several blocks away, walking across a vacant lot, when a pack of roaming mongrel dogs came out from behind an abandoned warehouse. At first, neither child thought anything of it. They knew dogs. Reservations and villages were full of dogs. But then the stray dogs saw them and ran straight at them, stopping short, barking at them, growling and baring their yellow teeth—slobber whipping across their snouts, their ears laid back against their mangy heads.

Lucy was frightened. She clutched Noah's arm. But Noah wasn't afraid. He stepped toward the angry animals, knelt on the brittle, dry grass, and held out a hand with his palm turned upward. He spoke to them softly in a sing-song fashion. The dogs stopped their menace, twitched their ears forward, and closed their teeth-filled mouths. One by one, they crept forward on their bellies, inch by inch, while the smiling boy spoke to each one, still holding out his open hand.

Lucy stood behind him, watching in amazement as the dogs smelled his palm, licked it, and then came in close and licked his face while Noah petted each one, stroking the matted coats of their backs and bellies. After a while he stood up, pointed in the direction they had come, and told them to go home. And although the dogs had no home, had no people who fed them, they trotted back across the empty field and disappeared behind the abandoned building.

Noah stood up, brushing dirt and grass from his knees.

"We'd better get back," he said, noting the low sun. Neither of them had a watch.

The two young Indians walked quickly back toward the station, side by side, passing carefully remembered storefronts and street signs. Lucy pulled the candy bar from her pocket, opened it, broke it in two pieces, and handed the bigger half to her new friend.

"That was scary," she said as they crossed the quiet street to the station.

Noah looked down at Lucy and smiled, and in that single smile she knew they had never once been in danger.

Ten minutes later, the half-empty bus left on schedule.

For the rest of the uneventful night and through much of the next day, the gray bus crossed over rivers and creeks, crawled across wide farming valleys, crept up hills and mountains on its long southeasterly journey. Passengers came and went and towns blended into one another. In all that time, Lucy and Noah talked and slept and laughed and cried and shared Noah's grocery bag of food. And with every passing mile, the boarding school loomed ever closer in the steadfast distance.

THE TRAIN CAR was stifling and poorly ventilated, and Simon Lone Fight was hot, sad, and hungry. He could at least do something about the heat: open the window beside his seat. Occasionally, he went into the small bathroom to wet his shirt. Wringing out the excess water, he'd put the soggy shirt back on and for half an hour would feel cool until the shirt dried out again. He could do something about the sadness, sleeping curled up on one of the worn seats, which were almost wide enough to accommodate three sitting passengers. With sleep came forgetfulness, driving the fear and sadness out of his immediate thoughts. In his dreams, red canyons passed softly beneath his feet, eagles soared in a blue sky beneath a yellow sun, and his shadow slouched against a canyon wall, catching its breath, its long black hair hanging nearly to the ground, waving him on to keep going.

In his peaceful, if strange, dreams, no long train headed northeast, and no parentless boy had been taken from his home. Instead, he felt the sure-footedness of his feet running across familiar earth, along with the constant rhythm, the drumbeat of his heart.

But nothing he could do would make the hunger go away. After so many jerking miles, the hunger built up inside him, and although one of the passenger cars was a diner, Simon had been given no money to buy food. Not a dollar. Like his belly, both pockets were empty. When he asked one of the porters how far it was to the town printed on his ticket, the man said it would be at least two days. On hearing the news, his shriveling stomach rumbled. What good was it that the conductor knew where he was supposed to go? What good was it that he "was not alone," according to the government man?

Two days would be too long.

That night after most of the passengers had long since gone to supper, Simon made his way forward through three passenger cars—the first and third full of double-wide passenger seats, all facing forward, the second a lounge car with tables and magazine stands and skylights in the ceiling—to the dining car, which was nearly empty. He could see a few people sitting at tables toward the middle of the car and, at the far end, what looked like a family of four. A waiter was cleaning tables toward the front and moving steadily toward the back. The car smelled of cigarettes and smoke from the greasy grill. The Indian walked slowly up the aisle, glancing at table tops, looking for leftover food. Spying an uneaten roll on one table, Simon grabbed it and slid it in his pocket before the waiter turned around. On another table half a steak lay in its cool, white-laced congealing juice. He grabbed it, too. Simon smiled when he passed the waiter.

"I was just looking for my parents," he said to throw off suspicion.

As the waiter resumed collecting dirty dishes in a gray, plastic container, Simon walked to the far end, smiling at the family members—a father, mother, and twin daughters—who were just finishing their meal. He could see that one of the little girls had not eaten all of her fried chicken. An untouched drumstick lay on the plate beside a pile of peas. He hoped they would leave soon and that the waiter wouldn't beat him to it. When Simon sat at a nearby table, the waiter asked if he wanted to order something.

"My parents said they'll meet me here soon," he said, smiling. "I'm just waiting."

It worked, because the waiter went back to his business. When the family left, Simon snatched the piece of chicken, rolled it in a napkin, and tucked it beneath his shirt. He strolled casually out of the diner. Two cars away, in the observation-lounge car, he found an empty table, sat down, pried the roll open with his fingers, and made a sandwich of the cold steak. He ate the chicken for desert. After his little meal, the boy sway-walked back to the next passenger car and lay down across the seat where he had opened the window and fell asleep again, temporarily allowing his mind to wander all the way back to the reservation.

When he woke up, it was morning. Simon sat up and looked around, yawning. There were more people in the car, mostly men in hats, wearing gray or black suits, reading newspapers, talking to one another, or smoking cigarettes while looking out the windows. Then Simon noticed an Indian boy, about his age, sitting in the double seat across the aisle, his back to the window and with his legs stretched across the neighboring seat.

Looking toward Simon, the boy asked, "What's your name?"

Simon yawned again and scooted to the aisle-edge of the coarse-fabric seat.

"Simon. What's yours?"

"Elijah," the boy replied, leaning forward, holding out a hand.

"Where you headed?" As Simon put this polite question and before Elijah could answer, a man in a gray suit with a briefcase walked up the aisle between them.

By what seemed a remarkable coincidence, the boys were going to the same place, an Indian school in the east with heavy iron gates out front that were connected by an iron arch emblazoning a name neither could remember. They shook hands and as the rattling miles passed they talked about their lives and about where they were going. Simon learned that Elijah had been traveling for a day and a half longer than he had, switching trains twice.

Around noon they both agreed they were getting uncomfortably hungry.

56

"You got anything to eat?" Elijah asked, having long since eaten the food his father had provided him in a grocery sack.

Simon knew just the thing.

"No," he said, standing up. "But I know where we can get somethin'."

Elijah grabbed his tan knapsack and followed Simon to the dining car where they were able to sneak food whenever no one was looking. At the porter's earlier instruction, Elijah had stowed his suitcase in the luggage car. Once they snitched enough food, the boys made their way back to the same seats and sat across from each other, eating and looking out the window. It felt good to fill their bellies, but they both endured sadness as the passing miles compacted behind them, like a logjam separating them from their increasingly distant homes.

Elijah had a deck of cards stashed in his pack. He taught Simon how to play several games, and for the rest of the day and into the night they played cards to pass the time—Go Fish, Hearts, and a simplified version of rummy that Simon's grandmother had taught him. Two sisters, both about their age and both white, boarded the train and played cards with the boys until they got off a couple towns down the track. They were going to visit their grandmother for the weekend.

That night Elijah and Simon slept on seats across from each other while the train inched its way across the map of the continent, slowly bringing them ever closer to their unknown destination. One boy dreamed of running beneath a long sky toward a low sun and across red earth; the other dreamed of half-frozen rivers, things long since dead, and things yet to come.

The next morning, after the boys had dawdled over a breakfast of leftover biscuits and one cold and limp piece of bacon, the train stopped at a busy station in a large city. The platforms were crowded with people, the sounds of their many voices and footsteps echoing in the porcelain light of the cool, gray morning.

A black porter came by and told them this was the end of the line.

"Ya' gotta get off now, boys," he said, without looking at their tickets. "Go on inside and they'll tell ya'll which train to take next. That man in the blue uniform, over there, he'll tell ya' what you need to do. Make sure to mind him."

The station was the largest building either boy had ever seen. It seemed big enough to hold every person in the world and most of the animals, too. Inside, at the ticket counter, a fat man behind a window told them which train to take. He told them what time it would depart and from which platform. The boys sat on one of the long wooden benches beneath the high, vaulted ceiling. The man in the blue uniform eyed them, then pulled out a small notebook and wrote something. Finally, he walked over to where the boys were sitting.

"You boys know where you're going?" he asked.

"Yessir . . . uh, no sir," Simon answered, showing the man the folded piece of paper that told him the name of the town for the school.

The man read the paper and then looked up at a big board on the wall.

"Your train doesn't leave until one o'clock. Be sure you're here and don't miss it. Understand?"

"Yessir," both boys answered.

Simon looked at a big round clock on the wall. They had several hours to wait. Just beyond the cavernous structure with its high, arched ceiling, the boys could see the whole downtown district of the great city. Skyscrapers rose to the clouds and through them. Cars and trucks and buses passed on the busy street. The sidewalks were packed full of people. Even from inside, they could hear the city and smell it. Neither boy had ever been to such a place, though they had seen pictures of great cities in movies. Simon had watched *King Kong* at least five times. It was his favorite movie. This place looked like the steel and concrete and glass city in the film.

Wherever it was, whatever it was named, the restless city called to the fascinated boys, and they answered by stashing Elijah's suitcase in a coin-operated locker and then walking through the wide doorway into the noisy sunlight.

Elijah stopped to stare at the intimidating height of the surrounding buildings. He had to tilt his head way back to see the tops. Narrow slits of blue sky appeared between the high rises. A cloud floated quickly above the thin slice of daylight and briefly stole the sharp-edged shadows the buildings cast across one another. The amazed Indian imagined all the people working in offices behind the gleaming windows. He looked back to the busy street, saw all the people crossing at lights, coming and going in both directions—some just milling around looking into shop windows, others hailing taxis. They reminded him of spawning salmon, the way they congregate in the sea just beyond the emptying mouths of rivers at low tide, waiting for high tide, the signal to begin their mad rush upriver to lay eggs or to fertilize them before they die, their bodies slowly rotting inward from the outside.

Simon grabbed Elijah by the arm.

"Come on, let's go that way," he said excitedly, pointing uptown.

The Indians walked for blocks. It seemed like every time they stopped to look around, someone walking by would hand them some change. The boys didn't understand why people should be giving them money. To them, city people were just the friendliest in the world.

By the time they reached a man selling hot dogs from a street cart, the boys had enough change to buy two dogs with the works. The man piled on everything: brown mustard and catsup, cooked onions, steaming kraut, and hot chili. When the vendor was done piling on condiments, they could hardly see the dogs nestled in the hot, damp buns. The boys ate as they continued their city adventure, their smiling and amazed faces turning at each new sound, at each new motion. The day was perfect, warm with only a slight breeze. Caught up in the enjoyment of adventurous exploration, the boys were momentarily forgetful of their sadness.

Briefly, they were happy.

On one street corner, people were coming out of a hole in the ground. The sound of squealing brakes and the now-familiar sound of iron wheels on steel tracks cried out from the opening. Simon and Elijah ran down the steps, jumping two at a time, just missing a little old lady wearing a large, flowered hat and clutching a bright, yellow handbag.

Simon paid the toll with loose change left over after buying the hot dogs. They had no plan to ride in the mysterious underground trains. They couldn't take the chance of missing their real-world train. They only wanted to look around. Besides, it was cooler underground. To Simon, it was like being inside some of the caves back home, only the walls of these concrete caves were painted with graffiti that glowed beneath flickering fluorescent lights casting shadows behind the rows of pillars.

Four older boys, probably in their late teens, emerged from the far end of the platform. They were wearing black leather jackets, even though it was a warm day. Their hair was combed back, slick and dark. They walked toward the two young Indians, talking and laughing among themselves as they approached. Simon and Elijah slowed their pace and tensed as they noticed the approaching pack. The older boys suddenly noticed the Indians. They stopped when they were close, blocking the way.

Elijah tried to step around one of the boys, but the older boy moved to block his path.

"Hey," the tallest of the four said. "You guys ain't from around here."

Simon spoke first. "We're just looking around," he replied, nervously.

The one who looked to be the oldest of the boys spoke next. "What are you guys, Mexican or something? Got any pesos?"

The other three laughed.

Elijah took a step forward. "We're *Indian*!" he said, his voice defiant, even prideful yet apprehensive.

One of the other boys grabbed the strap of Elijah's backpack.

"What ya' got in here?" the boy asked, yanking the strap so hard that he pulled Elijah off balance.

Elijah turned his shoulder hard, breaking the older boy's grip on the strap.

"Stuff," he said. "Nothing you'd want."

All four boys came closer to Elijah, encircling him, cutting him off from Simon, the way a wolf pack cuts off the too old, the too young, or the too sick from a herd. They were a pack—a pack roaming the undercity, a kind of wilderness.

"Give it to us," they demanded.

Elijah was scared. But then, suddenly, he saw the vague image of a man standing beside one of the boys, as if the stale platform air had taken shape. The man was gray and out of focus. His dirty white shirt was open for the first two or three buttons below the collar. A black tie hung loosely around his neck. He looked drunk. His eyes were dark and sad and empty, and his hair was messed. He had a bottle in one hand, a belt in the other.

Elijah spoke to the boy standing beside the apparition.

"You're going to end up just like your father," he said, matter-of-factly.

"What are you talking about?"

"Your father died from drinking too much. He beat you all the time."

The boy was visibly shaken. His face turned pale, and his voice quivered.

"How . . . how do you know about my old man?" he demanded.

The other boys, Simon included, didn't know what to do. They stood in the echoing cavern of the subway listening, goose bumps rising on their arms.

"He beat the hell out of you with a baseball bat, didn't he?"

"How do you know about that!" the older boy screamed above the screeching of an arriving train. The hissing doors opened; a few people got off while some people got on.

Elijah's voice was calm now, almost trance-like, even sad.

"He beat you when he was drunk, but you didn't deserve it. It wasn't your fault."

Tears welled up in the older boy's eyes.

"Shut up!" he shouted, knocking Elijah down to the dark, green-tiled floor.

"It wasn't your fault," Elijah said again, standing up.

A man at the far end of the platform yelled in their direction, and when the pack turned to look, Simon grabbed his friend by the arm and pulled him along.

"Run," he whispered.

That was the one thing Simon did better than anyone else. The one thing he knew could keep him safe. He ran.

They hadn't run a dozen steps when the pack gave chase. Simon poured it on. He ran as fast as he could, flying up the subway stairs three steps at a time. He ran down the street, passing yellow taxi cabs, a furniture delivery truck, a garbage truck, and pedestrians watching in disbelief. When he was two blocks away, he turned to his friend, laughing.

"That was close," he said.

But Elijah wasn't there. Simon had run too fast. Without thinking, he had unintentionally left his friend behind. Simon walked back down the busy street, but Elijah wasn't there. He made his way back to the subway entrance, but still he didn't see his friend. He crept down the steps, cautiously looking out for the pack. From the bottom of the steps he saw the four boys standing over Elijah on the nearly empty subway platform. They were rifling through his knapsack. Every time he tried to stand up, one of the boys shoved him down or kicked him in the side. A shabby, elderly woman was standing near a trash bin shouting at the boys to stop their bullying, but they ignored her.

"That's mine!" Elijah was yelling, reaching for his pack. It was clear even from the stairs that Elijah was crying. Anger mounted inside Simon. It was anger born of frustration and helplessness, the kind of pent-up anger many of the young men back on the reservation harbored deep inside. It grew so immense that it displaced the sadness he felt from being taken from his home. Without even thinking, he bounded down the stairs and jumped on the back of the closest boy, pounding on the side of his greasy head.

"Get him off me!" the boy screamed, spinning with the weight of the angry, young Indian on his back, Simon's long black hair sloshing back and forth.

The other boys joined in. They peeled Simon from the back of their fellow, like a tenacious strip of Indian Velcro. Once Simon was on the ground they started kicking him. Elijah stood up and shoved one of the boys. The unanticipated assault caught the boy off guard, and he tripped and fell. Things went badly for Simon and Elijah after that, simply a matter of mathematics. The four boys were much older, bigger, taller, and heavier. Besides, their lives had offered them an abundance of street-fighting experience, and their thick leather jackets reduced the impact of the smaller boys' punches. In no time, both Indians lay on the cold floor, tired and defeated.

One of the bullies grabbed Elijah's tan knapsack and poured out its contents in a shattering.

"There's nothin' in here but pictures," he said, bending over a heap of broken glass and twisted picture frames.

As they walked away down the poorly lit platform, two or three of the pack boys smoothed back their hair with their palms. Another was running a long, black comb straight back through his mop, depositing the comb, when finished, in his hip pocket.

Simon stood up first, offering Elijah his hand.

"We'd better get going," he said.

After replacing the contents in the knapsack, the boys walked up the stairs, their arms thrown over each other's shoulder, their free hand nursing aches and bruised ribs.

Neither spoke again until they were several blocks from the subway entrance, the train station looming in the distance.

"Don't worry," Simon said, his lower lip bleeding slightly. "You still got the pictures. That's what matters."

Elijah smiled, his left eye slowly swelling closed and darkening with deepening shades of blue, violet, purple.

Half an hour later their train rolled out of the shadowy station into the bright sunlight. The two boys sat across a table from each other playing cards, pausing occasionally to massage bruises gently and to look out the window as the teeming city gave way to slower-paced suburbs and finally to tranquil, flat countryside, the vanishing point of the iron tracks stretching toward their future.

Chapter Three

THE BLUE-FACED SILVER BUS slowed to a stop. Over the preceding two days, it had collected more and more Indian children, in towns and cities along the bus's long route. By the time it arrived at this destination, more than half the passengers were Indian.

Noah Boyscout looked out the window.

It was beginning to rain.

"Last stop!" the bus driver shouted, pulling the door lever and looking in the rear view mirror. "All you Indian kids gotta get off here!"

More than two dozen boys and girls stepped off the bus and gathered in the drizzle, looking up and down the wet road.

"Now what?" one boy asked, looking up at the driver, reaching to close the door.

"See them buildings over there?" he replied, nodding his head in the direction of a large complex of buildings on a slight hill. "That's your school."

As the anxious children picked up their bags and began to shuffle in the direction of the buildings, a train blared its arrival. Everyone turned. A long train was pulling to a stop alongside a small covered platform two hundred yards down the road from where they had disembarked from the bus, which was disappearing around a gentle distant curve in the road. The train came to

65

a full stop, and a hundred or more Indian children stepped onto the platform, milling around until they began to march toward where Noah Boyscout and Lucy Secondchief and the other bus passengers stood. Some carried suitcases, some duffel bags, and some nothing at all.

Some of the younger children were crying, the older ones comforting them.

Buses and trains had been stopping all day and even the day before to unload children, gathered from almost a hundred different tribes across the country.

The crowd from the train joined the small group from the bus, and together they walked alongside a high, redbrick wall until coming to the school's gate. Noah and Lucy stopped and looked up, the shuffling line of students passing around them. A beautiful, young woman wearing high heels that clicked on the cobblestone smiled at them as she passed. They wondered if she was a teacher. The imposing gate framed the view of the school beyond it. On each side rose a supporting square pillar of dark, reddish-brown bricks, the edges worn smooth from decades of rain. The pillars were tall, perhaps eight feet high, and a black iron arch spanned the cobbled walkway. The name of the school was spelled out in the middle, as if written by an iron finger.

Wellington.

Noah recognized the gate from the photograph the government man had showed him and his parents in their small cabin.

Although neither knew it at the time as they shuffled beneath the gate, for the rest of their lives Lucy and Noah and every new student in that slow-moving mass of drenched and somber children would know Wellington by a different name. Every Indian boy and girl who attended came to know the school as *Wekonvertum*. The mock-Indian term arose from what the children themselves came to understand as the purpose of the school: to "convert" not so much from ignorance to knowledge as from red to white, from citizens of home to citizens of a larger, more powerful culture, useful citizens of an overconfident nation.

Between the gate and the first closely grouped buildings, the way led across from a cemetery, clearly demarcated by a low iron fence. Noah detoured off the cobblestone path and toward the cemetery as he walked slowly up the hill, drawing close enough to read the names on many of the headstones. Some were very old, some new, the chiseled names and dates soft and vague or sharp and crisp, depending on the age of the slowly weathering stones. The simple markers were all about the same size, each about two feet in height, but they varied in width and thickness, due both to age and to slight design differences. Some of the stones bore only first names, some both names, mostly only surnames. Each included the name of a tribe: Sioux, Apache, Sac and Fox, Crow, Alaskan, Shoshone, Cherokee, Oneida, Creek, Eskimo, Hopi, Navajo, Ojibwa, Pueblo, Mohawk, Seneca, Chippewa, Cheyenne, Winnebago, Onondaga, Choctaw, Seminole, Shawnee, Iroquois, Osage.

There were hundreds of them.

The names, as Noah was later to learn, were of Indian children who had died at the school over the long years, mostly in the early days from rampaging and poorly treated diseases to which the Indians had no previous exposure or immunity. They died mostly from influenza, trachoma, small pox, or tuberculosis, which was the worst. A diagnosis of TB was a death sentence.

The government blamed the epidemic on the Indians' physical inferiority, even though it was they who brought the diseases to the children.

A gray squirrel scampered down an old massive oak tree, the only tree in the graveyard, searching for food among the dead. The tree was far older than the school, older than the laws that permitted this sad procession of children. It had witnessed more than the entire history of the nation.

Noah trotted back to join the group and Lucy, who was trembling, holding her arms tightly across her chest for warmth. He looked around at the hundreds of Indian boys and girls standing in the long line slowly shuffling toward the first building. There were almost as many children in the trudging mass as there were headstones in the cemetery.

Somewhere in the line ahead, Noah could hear crying.

At the top of the slight hill, toward the center of the institution's grounds, large buildings constructed of red bricks loomed in the drizzly overcast. The architecture was efficient, enduring, and depressingly institutional to the two young Indians. Broad, well-kept lawns separated the buildings from one another. A wind dragged itself with fistfuls of newly fallen leaves across the lawns. The air was chilly, and the distant structures, though massive, seemed to offer little reassuring warmth. Even the smoke billowing from the tall chimneys looked like cold, gray winter clouds.

A boy just behind Noah asked, "How'd you get here? I was on the train."

"We were on the bus," Noah replied, trying to be friendly.

Then a girl standing nearby joined their conversation.

"I started off in the back of a truck. There were maybe forty of us in the back of this truck. There wasn't even room enough to sit down. It was really cold, and everyone got hungry. Some of the kids had sack lunches and they shared. But most of us didn't get a sack. The truck didn't even stop to let us go to the bathroom. They just drove on and on. Finally, we were put on that train back there," she said, turning around and pointing downhill in the general direction of the train platform.

A boy in line ahead of them turned and joined the discussion.

"I was in the bottom of a ship for two days. It was dark and they didn't let us out, neither. It was like we was cows or something. They just herded us in and closed the door."

68

Lucy and Noah were glad that their travels had involved less physical suffering.

They felt blessed.

By now, the mass of young humanity was bunching up before the door to the first big building, where some staff were organizing things at the entrance. Every now and then the line moved forward a couple steps.

Lucy and Noah stood for a long time until their turn finally came to walk through the double doors of the administration building. They could feel heat pouring out the door, and they were glad to have made it inside. Posters dotted the wall. Most of them had a background formed of the American flag, with some patriotic slogan printed across it: *Home of the Free, Land of the Brave;* or *America the Beautiful;* or *With Liberty and Justice for All.* But one poster, by far the largest, simply had two words, without any flag, printed in large red letters. Just two words.

English Only.

The line of new students curved around a corner, but from its invisible front, they could hear the voices of school officials. Within minutes, Lucy and Noah were at the front of the line, standing before an elderly woman with tightly curled gray hair who asked them their last names.

"Boyscout," Noah replied. "This is Lucy Secondchief," he continued, placing one hand on the girl's shoulder.

"You go to the first line," the old woman said, pointing to the closest of several long tables arranged across the room, two women sitting stiffly behind one. "The girl goes to the end."

Lucy didn't move.

"Go on now," the woman demanded, her voice firm though practiced, not angry but without apparent feeling.

Noah leaned down and whispered to Lucy.

"It's okay. I'll be right over there."

At the front of the first long tables, a woman asked Noah his name again, while another woman rifled through a registry, her finger dragging down the page until she found his name.

"Boyscout. Here it is," she said checking off his name and then looking up. "Ninth grade. You'll be housed in Lathrop Hall. Please remember that name. Lathrop Hall."

The woman rifled through a folder and pulled out a form with Noah's name already typed across the top.

"Take this form and go to the next room at the end of the hall. Give it to the school nurse. She'll tell you what to do."

Noah walked over to Lucy and waited beside her. There were only two other people in front of her. She went through the same processing and was given the same form.

"Eighth grade," said a woman. "You'll be housed in Moore Hall. Please remember that name."

Together, they walked into the next room and stood at the end of another seemingly unmoving line.

While they waited, Noah looked at the form. It had all kinds of information about him: where he came from, which tribe, which reservation or agency, his mother's race, his father's race and occupation, how much land his family had been allotted by the government. It even offered a section on his health: height, weight, vision, vaccinations, hearing, and general fitness. Places were reserved for photographs and for teachers to write grades and remarks, which clubs he would belong to, and which trade skills he should learn.

Noah tried but failed to wrap his mind around that paper as his future. His mind remained as blank as the back of the complicated form.

When they came to the front of the line, Lucy and Noah were split up by gender, apparently to simplify the task of health officials in evaluating and marking their records. A long, white linen drape formed a separating wall, about seven feet tall—girls on one side, boys on the other.

The doctors and nurses tested the Indian children's eyes, making them read letters on a poster; gave them hearing tests, asking them to raise their left or right hand when they heard variously pitched beeping sounds; measured heights and measured weights; asked them to cough, to hold their breath. They checked scalps for lice and fleas and gave them a battery of vaccinations against polio, tuberculosis, measles, and tetanus. They tested their reflexes, examined their eyes and ears, and took temperatures and blood pressures, all the while writing numbers and remarks on the records of the quiet, unresisting children.

The enrollment process worked with remarkable efficiency. It had been refined over decades. So well-considered was every station of the process that none of the children seemed pressed to ask questions. And none of the staff found it necessary to speak to the children, other than to instruct them in an examination procedure or to request information.

At the end of the testing, a short man in thick, black-framed glasses collected the forms from the passing children and told them, in groups of eight or ten, to go straight through the back doors to the building on the other side of the parade field. He pointed to the building as he told them to stay on the walks and not to trample the lawn. To each small group he concluded in the same way, in the same practiced tone, "It's the cafeteria."

Lucy and Noah were hungry. They had spent most of the day standing in one line or the other, their resentful stomachs growling louder and louder.

The cafeteria was an expansive, open space filled with long tables and chairs. A bank of high windows ran along two walls. One of the ubiquitous "English Only" posters was fixed to the wall inside the entrance. A directing arrow mounted on a small wooden pillar just inside the door pointed to the serving area, which was preceded by stacks of plastic trays and a table with flatware, plates, and napkins. Another arrow pointed to a row of servers, all dressed in white, scooping meatloaf, white beans, and cabbage with long, metal ladles from heavy pots. None of the servers spoke to the children holding their plates out before them. At the end of the serving row stood a table with stacks of sliced white bread and pale margarine.

Lucy had never seen so much food. She only knew her meager diet of scrawny rabbits and wild Indian potatoes. Then she noticed the basket full of red apples, and she suddenly remembered the dream she had shared with her mother, the Indian boys and girls sitting at the table full of food.

Goose bumps raised on her arms.

Noah and Lucy both grabbed extra slices of bread and an apple and cautiously made their way across the room—careful not to spill the contents of their trays—to an almost empty table at the far end. They sat across from two boys about their age. Both had already eaten most of their supper. Each table was provided with yellow-plastic pitchers of milk and blue-plastic pitchers of water. As the children ate amid an increasingly noisy din of talk and clatter, young Indian girls, dressed in white aprons, continuously walked about replacing empty pitchers with full ones.

After eating just enough of the colorless food to tamp down his hunger, Noah looked up at the two boys sitting across from them.

"My name is Noah. I'm a freshman," he said, smiling as he wiped his chin. "This here's Lucy. She's in eighth grade."

The two boys nodded and smiled across the heavy wooden table.

"My name's Simon. This is Elijah. We're also freshman."

The four sat for a long time finishing their meals and talking about their adventurous journeys to the school. They all commented on how Simon's shiny, black hair was almost as long as Lucy's.

"Simon Longhair," Lucy said, half in fun, half in admiration. "I think it's wonderful."

An announcing voice came over the loudspeaker saying that the cafeteria would soon close. The man's monotone directed the children to check in at their assigned dormitory. The voice said that if any student had already forgotten which dormitory had been assigned, he or she could consult a list posted on the wall in the front of the cafeteria. Only Noah remembered his dorm. The other three needed to check the list.

On the way out the front door, Simon accidentally bumped into a larger, older Indian boy carrying his loaded tray toward an empty table. The impact sent the tray crashing to the shiny floor.

"Gee, I'm sorry," Simon said, his voice sincere.

"Why don't you watch where you're goin'?" the older boy yelled as he shoved Simon.

One of the older boy's friends came up beside him. Both had obviously been at the school for several years. They were juniors, near the top of the class hierarchy. Both wore letter jackets displaying their role as members of the football team.

"Pick it up," the first boy commanded.

Simon knelt down and picked up the tray in one hand, collecting the silverware with the other. He stood up, holding the tray.

"What about the food on the floor?" the boy said, looking down at the mess. "I'm not going to clean it up."

His friend jumped into the taunting.

"You clean it up," he said. "Eat it off the floor."

Simon looked at both of them and then down at the mishmash of food splattered on the polished floor.

"Go ahead," the second boy said again. "Eat it."

Noah, Elijah, and even Lucy stood by Simon. Noah spoke first.

"He said he was sorry. It was an accident."

Elijah joined in. "Yeah, it was just an accident."

Little Lucy came and stood directly in front of Simon, looking up at the two older boys, knitting her black eyebrows together in an effort to look menacing.

"He said he was sorry," she said sharply, her little fists clenched.

The boy who had carried the tray shoved Lucy aside and grabbed Simon by the shirt. He had drawn back a balled-up fist when two staff members came by and broke up the squabble, calling the older boys by their last names.

"Highmountain! Lame Deer!"

The adults sent the four young friends away while keeping the older boys behind to speak to them about their behavior to under-classmen. When Simon was safely out of the cafeteria and standing before the list of dormitory assignments posted on the outer wall of the hallway, just to the right of the door, he turned to his group of new friends and quietly thanked them for standing by him.

All of them, even little Lucy, patted Simon on the back or shoulders.

Sometimes it takes people years to make friends. Sometimes the best friends are made swiftly, in an instant rather than over weeks or months. All four children seemed to gather that at a place like Wellington, the closest friends are sometimes those made early on. Certainly, they would get to know one another better in the days and months and years to come, but all four already felt a bond.

A map of the campus was posted beside the dormitory assign-ment list. By happy coincidence, all three boys were assigned to the same dorm, Lathrop Hall, but Lucy was assigned to Moore Hall, which was appointed for girls. The boys agreed to escort Lucy to her dorm first, and then they walked two buildings over to their own. The sun was just setting behind the farthest build-ing when they walked through the heavy double doors of their new home.

In the center of the well-lit lobby two older men sat behind a long table.

"Names!" one of the men called as the three boys walked to-ward the imposing table.

Elijah saluted and announced the names: "High Horse, Lone Fight, Boyscout," while the old men slowly and methodically looked up and down their long lists ticking off the names. They gave the boys their room assignments. Though all were different rooms, all three were on the same floor.

The balder of the two men announced to the boys a summary of instructions. "Your floor monitors will go over the house rules at 8 p.m. Until then, you are free to inspect your rooms, but you may not leave the building."

The man said nothing more after that. He simply turned and pointed toward the wide staircase behind him, one of those "English Only" posters pasted to the wall on the first landing.

At the floor meeting, held for the benefit of new and returning students alike, the residents were given a variety of instructions, everything from curfew hours, to how to make a bed, to how long to shower. There were strict rules against taking long showers. The floor monitors warned them not to speak their Native languages or to dance Indian-style dances or to do anything Indian. After dismissal, the boys all went to their assigned rooms for the night. Each room was the same, each framed within dark-paneled walls. Each was supplied with a single small window, two beds, two desks, and two small closets. On each narrow bed rested a pillow, a stack of neatly folded sheets, a dark blue blanket, and two white towels.

Whenever the steam heat kicked on, the radiator in every room made fitful popping and hissing sounds.

All the new boys and girls slept restlessly, tossing and turning, kicking at their stiff sheets, dreaming of home, wherever that home had been. Late into the night, while the children slept, the staff readied themselves for the year to come, the kitchen staff sharpening their knives, the faculty sharpening their lesson plans, all of them sharpening their skills at instructing without conversing, supplanting any sense of compassion with the sense of purpose.

Chapter Four

THE SECOND DAY at Wellington began with the usual commotion of boarding school: floor monitors calling out and banging on dorm room doors, some students crying after waking up and realizing where they were, kitchen staff stacking plates and preparing breakfast, the JROTC units shouting out cadence songs as they jogged and slogged around the sodden track half asleep, each young cadet trying to keep rhythm in the half-dark.

Within thirty minutes all the children had washed, dressed, straightened their rooms, and made their uncomfortable beds, the corners tightly tucked as they had been instructed the night before. The floor monitors told the boys to assemble at the main administration building in five minutes, the first building they had entered the day before, where they had been examined and prodded by health officials.

When Elijah, Simon, and Noah arrived at the building, almost a hundred boys were already standing in line in front of the dark, thick doors.

The drizzle had stopped during the night, but the morning was still cold and gray and wet.

It was almost an hour before Simon, Noah, and Elijah had passed through the doors, wound around the corner, and come within view of their destination. They could see the line turning into a brightly lit room about halfway down the long hall.

They wondered at the buzzing, electrical sound that began to drift from the room. Occasionally, the lights overhead flickered on and off. Eventually, after much speculation, they could see into the buzzing room. A dozen chairs were placed in two neat rows. At each chair a solemn barber was shaving a distraught Indian boy's head, the hiving sound of electric hair clippers echoing against the high walls and closed windows. A stern, gray-suited, stolid woman with chin whiskers and gray hair stood at the end of the line, pointing to vacant chairs whenever a barber was done.

"Next!" she'd shout, leading a boy by the arm and pointing across the loud room.

A door was propped wide open at the far end. Through it a single-line stream of boys steadily passed, each rubbing a hand across a newly shaven scalp, all of a death-gray tint of skin unused to light. From a distance, they all looked the same. Two older Indian boys, both seniors, stood on either side of the door.

When the three young friends came to the front of the line, panic began to well up inside Simon. His heart began to race. His stomach felt so tight that he thought he might vomit. His mother always loved Simon's long hair. His father was always proud of it, saying what a good little warrior Simon was. His long hair wasn't just part of his appearance; it was part of who he was.

Simon stepped behind Noah and Elijah, buying time. When the whiskered woman finally indicated that it was his turn, Simon darted across the bustling room toward the open door.

But before he made it, the two seniors caught him and dragged him back to an empty chair, holding his arms, twisting them painfully behind his back as Simon screamed his terror. He wriggled in the chair, trying to break free, but the two boys held him fast while the barber did his job, handfuls of shiny, black hair tumbling down his arms and back, spilling onto the growing heap of hair already lying on the smooth floor of shiny black-and-white linoleum tiles.

Simon screamed so loudly that boys still behind in the hallway lines thought surely someone was dying. Everyone stopped to see what the commotion was. Barbers held their idle electric clippers in their idle hands, curious boys still in line edged close together trying to peek into the room, along the outside wall of the building, boys, including Noah and Elijah, and groundskeepers stood tippy-toed trying to look through the windows.

Crows lifted out of the great oak in the cemetery, and song birds stopped singing.

The sky began, once again, to drizzle.

While the electric clippers sheared his hair, Simon closed his eyes, trying to make it all go away like a bad dream, trying to make Wellington go away. He thought about home on the reservation and about his grandparents, trying desperately to replace the moment with happier thoughts.

LUCY SAT ACROSS FROM SIMON at breakfast. Simon did not speak the entire time, quietly staring at his plate, tears occasionally dripping onto his pancakes. Elijah and Noah didn't know what to do or say. After a while, Lucy reached across the table and held his hand. She squeezed it firmly but said nothing. Simon raised his head, and Lucy saw the despair in his eyes, saw it lying there like a still, black pool. Suddenly, she too began to cry. Outside, the drizzle picked up its pace, and the low, gray clouds burst open, releasing a torrent of rain. The winds gusted, the few trees around campus bent double like old men, and every last leaf was torn from every limb until the trees, too, looked shorn and naked. The fall was disappearing and making room for the coming winter.

Noah asked Lucy how her first night went. All three of her friends awaited her reply, but the question made her nervous. She looked down at the table, pulling a wadded strand of her hair.

Finally, she looked up and whispered, "I overheard some of

the other girls talking before bedtime. They were talking about how sometimes male staff members or teachers sneak into a girl's room late at night. They were talking about what happened to some of the girls last year."

The boys could tell that Lucy was worried.

After discussing the problem for a while, the boys thought of a way to help protect their friend. Finally, they agreed that she could snatch some empty cans from the cafeteria's garbage bin, peel off their labels, wash them, and stack them neatly against her door so that they would fall over in a clamor should someone try to enter her room at night. Elijah thought for a moment and then warned Lucy she would have to explain things to her roommate, who might otherwise accidentally trigger the makeshift alarm going to the bathroom in the middle of the night. The three boys laughed, leaving Lucy a little embarrassed at first.

The idea of the cans seemed to lessen Lucy's anxiety. Before they left the cafeteria's grounds, all four rifled through the dumpster. With her arms full of half a dozen cans, Lucy smiled for the first time since bedtime the night before.

The boys escorted her back to her dorm, where she hid the cans under her bed for the time being. Afterward, all four made their way across campus to the instruction building, where all students were given their semester class schedule. After that, the headmaster held convocation in the gym. The bleachers were packed with young Indians from all across the nation by the time the faculty solemnly took their places on the stage, all wearing long, black gowns, and their faces bearing no sign of anticipation or excitement. The headmaster spoke for almost an hour about patriotism and what it means to be a good American citizen. He talked about the importance of education and training. Even the faculty seemed uninterested in his droning voice. Noah nudged Simon and pointed to a teacher on the back row who was blatantly asleep; others of the faculty looked down at their hands folded neatly in their laps. To Simon, they looked like they wished they could be asleep, too.

Finally, the headmaster's speech was over. After the somber faculty marched out the double doors to the gym, all of the students emptied out and hurried to lunch, some racing to be first in line.

Lucy, Noah, Simon, and Elijah took their time, talking and even laughing as they made their way to the cafeteria, Simon occasionally dragging a hand across his shaved head in disbelief.

They had survived the long journey and the first day of school. What's more, they had made friends. They looked around at the stark buildings, at the tangled vines climbing up the dark, reddish-brown brick walls, at the broad fields, at the cemetery of dead children, and down toward the iron gates separating them from the world. The geography of their past lives, including their families, lay somewhere on the other side of the rusting gate. But however far it was to home, this place would be their home for the rest of the year, perhaps for many years to come.

The nameless days ahead were uncertain. None of the four friends felt certainty or hope or joy, but at least they took some consolation knowing they would not face their unwelcome future alone.

Chapter Five

LUCY HATED THE NIGHTS at wellington. Although she had been there nearly a month, she was still afraid to fall asleep, frightened by what the other girls whispered, about things that happened at the school at night. Even though her roommate, who was older than Lucy, tried to play down the rumors and whispers, Lucy remained frightened at night and insisted on maintaining her booby trap of tin cans.

She missed her tiny, sagging log cabin, the flavorless boiled rabbit, the after-supper conversations and stories, the crackling wood stove. It wasn't much to look at, but it was home. Mostly, she missed her mother's reassuring closeness beside her in their bed. She missed the way she smelled, the way she breathed quietly in the dark, the way she could feel her mother's warmth radiating from her side of the bed, piled heavy with blankets and quilts, the northern lights outside glimmering below the starlit spiral arm of the galaxy.

At Wellington, Lucy rarely fell asleep before midnight, and then only fitfully. Instead, she'd lie on her narrow, spring-infested mattress tossing and turning, listening, her eyes forced open despite the darkness, the lateness of the hour, and her body's need for recuperation.

Outside her booby-trapped door, strange sounds came from the hallway, from the stairs at the end of the hall, from outside her window, beneath the floor, above the ceiling, and from the bathroom three doors down. The floors creaked, the heating pipes groaned like lonesome ghosts, and vague voices echoed in the dark. Throughout the night she'd hear doors open and the sound of feet pitter-patting down the hall to the bathroom. Shortly thereafter, she'd hear a flush and the pipes would groan again. Every twenty minutes the heater would kick in, hissing and rattling as it heated up.

Sometimes the sounds would even awaken her roommate, Maggie Yazzie, who would stop her sometimes raspy breathing, turn over, and fall back asleep. Maggie was the most beautiful girl on the floor, maybe in the entire school. Although barely sixteen, she looked seventeen or eighteen. She was tall, with long black hair and jade-green eyes.

All the boys wanted to be with Maggie.

Some of the male teachers, too.

Lucy envied her self-confidence and popularity. Even though Maggie was older and seldom with Lucy during the day, for they had no classes in common, she was pleasant to Lucy while in their shared room, and Lucy began to think of her as a big sister.

Sometimes while lying awake at night, Lucy, in her paranoia, would think footsteps stopped just outside her door. She'd stare at the door knob until her mind played tricks, convincing her that the brass knob really was turning. In her sleepy mind's eye, she could see shadows under the door trying to wriggle into the room past her neatly stacked pyramid of tin cans.

For the most part, Maggie eventually convinced Lucy that such visions and fears were the product of an over-anxious imagination. But no matter the reality, the distressful stories lingered in Lucy's mind.

For almost an hour one night Lucy endured the need to relieve herself. She kept hoping the increasing discomfort would go away. But like the unsettling sounds, the pain persisted until she had to get up and go to the bathroom. She had heard some of the other girls speak of enduring the pain of a full bladder. To them, it was better to suffer than to walk alone through the long, dark hallway to the bathroom. On her knees, Lucy carefully dismantled her alarm system of empty cans, placing each one in a row beside her bed, a few feet from the door. She always took great care in this nightly ritual, not wanting to wake Maggie. Then, she slowly opened the door, looked both ways down the long, poorly lit hallway, and walked as quickly and as silently as possible in her cotton nightgown to the bathroom, located about midway between each end of the long, narrow corridor.

When she was finished, Lucy washed her hands and leaned close to the mirror on tiptoes looking at her face, her eyes, her eyebrows, the shape of her lips, her cheekbones, her thin-ridged nose, and her long hair. She wondered if the place had changed her somehow, if her mother would see the changes in her, would recognize her.

Looking both ways again, Lucy crept quietly back to her room, trying not to make the worn floorboards squeak.

When she came to her room, the door was ajar. Hadn't she closed it? Lucy stopped for a moment, trying to remember if she had. She replayed her earlier movements, clearly recalling the sharp click of the latch catching. But now the door was slightly open. Lucy pushed on it lightly. It swung inward with a slow, soft creaking.

A blade of the hallway's light pierced the dark room and cut across Maggie's bed. At its edge, a man hunched over her motionless form inside its cotton nightgown, one hand under the dark blue blanket. Startled, the man swung his face toward the sound and light and saw Lucy standing in the doorway. He jumped to his feet and lunged toward the girl. Without even thinking, Lucy jerked the door closed and ran down the hall to the stairs at the nearer end of the hallway, while back in the room the man fumbled in the darkness feeling for the doorknob. In his haste, he kicked some of the tin cans across the room, waking Maggie who sat up in her bed.

"Who's there?" she called out in her half-sleep.

Enough moonlight poured into the room so that she could barely make out the shape of a tall man. She screamed just as he twisted the doorknob and sprinted out of the room. Maggie jumped up and rushed to Lucy's bed.

"Wake up, Lucy," she shouted, probing amid the disheveled blanket for her roommate.

DOWNSTAIRS IN THE LOBBY, Lucy tried to open the front doors, but they were locked. She pushed uselessly against the handle until she heard the sound of someone coming down the staircase. In a panic, she looked around the large room, trying to find some place to hide. But the spacious, open lobby provided no concealing cranny, no large furniture. As quietly as possible, she ran down one of the two halls that led from the lobby. At the end of the hall was a large window and when Lucy lifted, it rose stiffly in its peeling-paint sash. By hiking up her white cotton night shirt, she managed to crawl out the window, drop to the ground, and hide behind a bush at the corner of the building.

The rain had long stopped. The moon was full, and silvery light fell on the world, casting shadows. The sky was almost entirely clear, the moon so bright that only the brightest stars were visible. It was near freezing outside, but Lucy's shivering was not from the cold.

From her hiding place, she could see the man emerge from the front door. She wondered how he had opened the locked door. Did he have a key? Everything had happened so fast that she didn't get a good look at his face. From what she saw and remembered, she did not recognize him. Once outside, the man walked slowly in Lucy's direction, close to the wall of the building, occasionally stopping to look behind shrubs.

He was searching for her.

Lucy held her breath, trying to slow her heartbeat, trying to vanish altogether. She looked around for a better place to hide, but there was little between her dormitory and the next building, the gymnasium.

When he drew close to the building's corner, she bolted like a rabbit across the lawn toward the gym. The man, suddenly seeing her, ran after her, tripping and falling on an exposed tree root. Lucy heard him curse, and over her shoulder she could see the man scrambling back to his feet. When she had made it safely around the corner of the gym, she threw herself against the dark wall, catching her breath and peering around the corner. The man was midway across the lawn. In the half-dark, she could see that he was limping badly from the fall.

Looking around her, she saw the trees at the far edge of the football field, the beginning of a dense forest, about a mile square. It would be a long run across the playing field with nothing at all to hide behind. Even the grass was still short from the last mowing at the season's end. She peeked around the corner again and saw that the man was close, his limping gate aimed at Lucy's position.

With no remaining options, Lucy decided to dash across the wide, open field, certain she would be seen.

At that very moment, quiet as lust, a cloud—the only one visible in the entire night sky—slid under the moon like an umbrella, blocking most of the bright silvery light. It was a small cloud. It should have passed quickly beneath the moon, but it seemed to be fixed in the sky, in such a way that no light fell in pure rays on the dewy field, on the distant forest, or on the little, desperate girl running.

When the man finally made it to the back of the gymnasium, the field before him was dark. Everything around him was dark. In the inkwell of that night, he leaned heavily against the brick wall with one hand, rubbing his wrenched ankle with the other.

The man looked along the wall of the building, then back toward the dorm, and finally out into the dark field, concluding that toward the football field and the woods beyond was the only direction the girl could have run. Yet he saw nothing moving on the field, could barely make out its edge at all.

He shuffled uncertainly toward the field as the small cloud's edge drew close to the hiding moon, its light beginning to spill over the small cloud's brim. Just as the field began to reappear in the moonlight, a motion from near the bleachers caught his eye. He stopped to watch as three deer, all does, stepped onto the turf cautiously, the way all deer betray their nervousness. They started for the middle. The man looked back toward the buildings, and then to the left and right of where he stood. But there was no sign of the girl. When he looked back to the field, the deer were standing in the middle, between him and the dark woods, between him and Lucy's fleeing form. As if guided by a sense of geometrical precision, the deer blocked the girl's terrified escape from the man's angry eye. If they had stopped anywhere else, a few feet left or right, a few steps closer or further away, the man might have seen her. But for that exact instant, Lucy was invisible—shielded, as it were, by deer—as she raced across the field, trembling from fear and cold.

Confused about Lucy's whereabouts, the man cursed, shrugged his shoulders, turned, and shuffled away, favoring his right leg.

After he was gone, the nibbling deer moved on, their ears pricked for any sound, their lithe muscles tensed to jump at any motion. The little cloud moved on too, and the moon once again bathed the field fully in bright moonlight, pouring down on the tiny shape of the distant, barefoot girl as she entered the safety of the shadowy forest on the other side.

Afraid that she might be caught, Lucy huddled in some low bushes beneath a great tree, shivering all through the long night.

AFTER FINDING LUCY'S BED EMPTY, Maggie woke up

the floor monitor, who awakened the dorm mother, who called the headmaster. Everyone assumed that the intruder had abducted Lucy, that the perpetrator had entered the room on her account, that she, not Maggie, had been the target. Throughout the rest of the cold night, staff members searched the campus, calling out Lucy's name, the yellowish beams of flashlights bobbing up and down in the darkness. But huddled where she was beneath a tree in the woods across a field at the farthest edge of Wellington's grounds, Lucy never heard their shouts.

The whole school was in an uproar. Boys and girls in every dorm opened their windows to look out and listen. Noah, Simon, and Elijah heard the shouting. They heard the rumors about a young girl named Lucy and pleaded to join the search party, but they were not allowed. None of the students were allowed outside the dorms. They were told sharply to go back to their rooms. But the three boys were committed to finding their friend. All three pulled their bed sheets, met in Elijah's room, and tied the sheets together, forming a rope long enough to reach almost to the ground. They secured one end to a heater and, one by one, slid down the thick, knotted rope, crouching beneath a shrub when two teachers hurried by, shining their flashlights along the cobbled walk ahead.

After they passed, Noah stood up and signaled for the others to follow him, as he crept like a thief across the lawn separating the buildings.

When they arrived at Lucy's dorm, Noah walked slowly and carefully along the outside walls, pausing briefly beneath each window. At one open window he paused longer than he had at the others, his fingers feeling the soft earth.

He stood up and looked toward the gymnasium.

"She went that way," he said quietly as they took a few steps. "The strides are longer here. She was running. Somebody must have been chasing her."

The three boys raced to the gym. At the corner, Noah knelt down, studying the ground again. He stared at it intensely for almost a minute, his eyebrows knit tightly, trying to focus in the dark, looking first at the ground and then toward the football field.

"She went that way," he said, pointing at the field.

"How do you know that?" asked Simon.

Noah motioned both of them to kneel down close to the ground.

"See these footprints?" he asked, holding an open hand beside the tracks. "Can you tell anything about them?"

Elijah replied first. "They're bare feet."

Noah gently pressed his fingers into the shallow depression of the fresh tracks.

"I saw these same tracks under that window over at Lucy's dorm. Look how small they are. They're a small girl's. They were headed this way. She stopped here."

Both boys looked into Noah's face, smiled, and shook their heads.

"Damn, Noah!" Elijah said, full of admiration and sudden high spirits. "You're a real Indian!"

Noah chuckled. "Shut up, jerk."

Then, all three followed the tracks toward the football field, Noah in the lead, stopping periodically to kneel and examine the earth.

"She ran in that direction," he said, looking across the playing field toward the woods.

Halfway across the field, the boys came upon deer tracks, like the marks of small prongs jammed into the damp earth.

On the other side, the tracks of small bare feet led into the dark forest. Noah had difficulty reading the signs at first, but all three were sure Lucy was nearby. They pressed on through the dense undergrowth calling softly, "Lucy . . . Lucy."

They eventually found her shaking uncontrollably in the bushes beneath a great, old tree. Her teeth were chattering like a telegraph—her breath billowing like smoke signals. She was too cold to speak. Simon took off his warm jacket and wrapped it around Lucy's shoulders. Elijah covered her legs with his jacket. Noah draped his windbreaker over her like a blanket and placed his baseball cap on her head. They decided not to try to move her until they could warm her enough so that she could walk on her own.

While they sat with their quiet friend, the boys talked about all kinds of things.

Suddenly, Lucy said something so quietly no one understood what she had said.

"What'd you say? asked Simon, leaning closer, motioning for the other two boys to stop talking.

"To . . . to-day," said Lucy, her teeth chattering, "was my birth-day."

Lucy had turned fourteen and no one had even noticed. Most birthdays went unnoticed at Wellington. Indeed, all three boys would turn fifteen during the year, and even they wouldn't notice. What was there to celebrate at a place like Wellington other than leaving it?

The three boys huddled around Lucy until the sun braved the cold morning and stretched to look over the horizon. When it was light enough to see, all three helped Lucy up and led her out of the tangled forest, across the wet field, and past the gymnasium.

WORD OF THEIR RETURN SPREAD across the worried school like a fry-bread grease fire. Everyone ran out to greet them. The school nurse and an assistant came running out from a building and took Lucy to the infirmary, where they quickly warmed her body in a hot bath, giving her cups of hot tea.

The headmaster came and told the boys to wash up and join the rest of their dorm at breakfast. When they finally walked into the crowded and noisy cafeteria, everyone stopped talking. Several dozen children stood up and began to applaud. Then others joined in until every single person was standing and clapping. Even the kitchen staff came out from behind their kettles and serving stations to applaud.

It wasn't until lunch time that they saw Lucy again.

They carried her tray as they escorted her to their table and asked her why she ran away. Lucy told them about the man in her bedroom. She told them how he was sitting on Maggie's bed with one hand beneath her blanket. She told them how she didn't recognize the intruder, but how he fell during the chase and limped from the fall, favoring his right leg.

For the rest of the day, whenever they could meet, the boys walked around the school looking for a tall man with a limp. They put out the word to other children, who joined in the search. There had been many of these night visits over the years, and it wasn't always into the rooms of girls that some intruders crept. Most of the accosted girls, and all but a very few of the accosted boys, were too ashamed to tell anyone. The few who had complained to school officials were largely ignored. Some of the complaints were dismissed as understandable childish anxiety. Worse, some were dismissed or covered up as actual events that could cost notoriety, investigations, public concern, budget restrictions, and jobs.

By late afternoon, the boys thought that maybe they had found the man they were looking for. It was the choir teacher, a tall, thin, young man with stringy, light-brown hair. His name was Mr. Wilkinson. He had a reputation for flirting with the girls. Indeed, most of his students were girls. Every day he rode to school on his red and chrome motorcycle, wearing a black leather jacket and no helmet. Elijah spoke with one of the girls who was in the choir and also in Elijah's English class. She and another girl said that Mr. Wilkinson had developed a limp, which he did not have the day before. When Elijah shared this information with his two friends, they became pretty sure they had their man, but they wanted to be certain.

Noah watched Wilkinson leave his office for supper. Even faculty who lived off campus were required to eat lunch and supper at the school. Breakfast was optional. Faculty ate in their own dining hall adjacent to the cafeteria. After the tall, thin man had walked through a patch of soft ground, Noah studied the prints. Then he retraced Lucy's trail from the previous night. The man's shoe prints matched those following Lucy's exactly, including the deep gouge in the sole of the right shoe.

At supper, Noah shared with Simon and Elijah what he had found. The other two boys had also learned more about Wilkinson. Some of the girls had told them how he made unwelcome remarks about their clothes or their hair or the way they walked—even touching them in ways teachers should not touch students. Some girls admitted that he would take them into his office on some pretense of discussing grades or performance and kiss them. As the boys later learned, many of the girls went to choir feeling sick to their stomach, praying they weren't pretty enough to catch his attention. With suspicion now certainty, the boys worked out their plan.

The next evening, while all the students were still at supper, the three boys left and gathered in the faculty parking lot with a bundle of rope, block-and-tackle pulleys, a can of black paint, and a paint brush, all gathered from the automotive shop building, where the older boys were taught the rudiments of auto mechanics. The teacher, Mr. Weil, was from New Jersey. He was a stocky second-generation Irish-American, with balding red hair and a scruffy, red beard. He stayed as grimy as the engines he worked on, and he had a penchant to recite poetry at a moment's notice. But the boys who took his class liked him, not necessarily because he was a good teacher but because he taught one of the two things that most interested teenage boys, the other being girls. Almost every day after school, some of the boys would meet in the shop to help Mr. Weil work on cars, usually belonging to members of the faculty or staff. It was all under the table, of course. But, Mr. Weil always gave each boy who helped him a little money, which the boys, in return, used to buy cigarettes. Most of the older students at Wellington smoked, secretly, behind buildings, trees, hedges, bleachers, in the woods, or openly in Mr. Weil's shop class, a square pack rolled up in each boy's white T-shirt sleeve.

Noah's roommate was one of those boys and had told Noah how to get into the shop after hours.

When Noah, Simon, and Elijah were certain that no one was watching, they quickly pushed the choir teacher's motorcycle close to the base of the single, massive oak tree in the cemetery. Simon climbed up the tree and set up the block and tackle. He pulled one end of the rope through the two blocks of four pulleys, feeding it through until one end reached the ground and securely fastened the upper block to a stout limb. Elijah and Noah tied the rope around the motorcycle's frame, and pulling hard with all their combined weight, hoisted the heavy bike, inch by inch, high into the naked branches of the old tree. While his two friends held the rope taut by wrapping it around the base of the tree, Simon tied off the motorcycle with a short piece of rope, so that it would be more difficult to bring it down. Then he untied the upper block, replaced both in the sack, and dropped the longer rope, which fell to the ground in a loose pile.

Back in the cafeteria, they told all the students at one table what they had done. From there, the news spread fast, as if poured out from the many pitchers of water and milk, spilling throughout the room, finding the path of least resistance, like a river, to every Indian ear. When the choir teacher left the faculty dining hall that evening, all the students quietly filed out of the cafeteria, keeping a goodly distance behind the man who never once turned around. Their long shadows crept ahead of them, keeping close watch on the lone figure leading the curious mass to the parking lot. Wondering at the commotion, the kitchen staff left their posts, followed by all the teachers watching the procession outside the faculty dining-hall windows. As they marched across campus toward the parking lot, other staff members saw the line and joined the curious parade.

As the choir teacher passed through the cemetery on the cobbled walk, something caught his eye, a flashing high up in a tree. He stepped off the path onto the lawn, meandered around headstones until he stood at the base of the tree. He looked up and saw his motorcycle suspended high up in the great tree, the late evening rays of the setting sun reflecting off the chrome like a warning signal. Even from the ground he could see the word "pervert" painted on both sides of the fuel tank.

Shortly after, every boy and girl, every kitchen worker, grounds keeper, custodian, teacher, and administrator stood in a wide arch around the base of the gray tree, their faces turned upward in disbelief, staring at the red and chrome motorcycle, slowly spinning like a lie.

Chapter Six

SIMON COULDN'T FIGURE IT OUT. He stared at the paper lying on his desk, at the big capitalized letter D handwritten in red ink at the top left corner. He had worked on the paper for a week—really worked on it, even asking a couple of his friends to read it and to give their advice. He had revised it three times, checking spelling, inserting facts, altering phrasing. Everyone who read it, even though some offered corrections or suggestions, thought it was an A paper.

Everyone but Mr. Hand.

He was the new English teacher. He hated his job teaching freshman English at Wellington. He had been hired in a pinch when another teacher suddenly quit. He hated that he was surrounded by "minority" children, Indians, weaker students, he felt, than he deserved. He had taken the job at Wellington as an interim measure, until he could get a real job teaching real students at a real school.

"Indians." He sneered whenever he said the word, just like when he said "Nigro."

"The only thang worse than an Indian," he once told the class, "is a Nigro. God made y'all different from white folks. That's why y'all are here, because yo' brains aren't made the same as white folks. Y'all seem to have great difficulty understandin' things the way we do."

Mr. Hand was from the Deep South, so deep he believed Moses parted the Mississippi, his family used to the privilege of authority and respect.

When the short and balding teacher was looking away, Noah, delighted with his grade, held up his paper so that Simon could see his result, which was a B+. Simon had read Noah's essay. It wasn't better than his. It had lots of misspellings, and it never once quoted any facts from the textbook. It was full of fragments and even a page short of the requirement. By all accounts, Simon's paper was better, and yet it received a much lower grade.

Mr. Hand walked around the room, quietly returning essays, scowling frequently as he dropped papers on desks in front of frightened students. Simon motioned to several students sitting nearby.

"Whadya' get?" he whispered, leaning over.

One student got a B; another a C-. One had a D.

Simon turned around to face Willa Spotted Elk, a pretty halfbreed with blue eyes and light brown, almost ivory skin, which contrasted sharply against her long, shiny auburn hair. Her features were less Indian looking than most of the other girls in the class. Willa showed Simon her grade when the teacher wasn't looking.

It was an A.

"Can I look at it?" Simon asked, interested to see how much better her paper was than his own.

Willa nodded and Simon hurriedly lifted it from her desk top. He read the first page quickly, skimming mostly. The paper was terrible. It was much worse than Noah's. And yet, there perched the smiling red letter A at the top left corner, while a brooding D squatted on his own first page. He couldn't figure it out.

Mr. Hand finished passing out the marked essays.

"Next week we shall be reading Shakespeare. Now, I rather doubt that a group of Indians will be able to grasp the complexity of such a great playwright, but we shall read him anyhow. It's expected. We'll begin with *Hamlet*. You might actually enjoy it. It's kind of ghost story, if you will."

The bell rang while he was handing out cheaply printed copies of the play.

"Make sure you read through Act III by Monday," he yelled above the din of chairs sliding out from beneath desks.

Simon read *Hamlet*, the whole play, over the weekend. It was hard for him at first. The unfamiliar and archaic words and the strange phrasings confused him. But he quickly learned to read beyond the difficult language, letting the events of the story unfold. It didn't matter that the play was hundreds of years old. His own version of the story began to take shape in his mind. Instead of Elsinore, Wellington was the setting of Simon's version, and he filled it with dozens of Indian characters. In his mind, Lucy was Ophelia. Mr. Hand convincingly played the evil, brother-murdering King Claudius. Noah was Laertes and Elijah was Horatio, Hamlet's best friend. Naturally, Simon was Hamlet. He became absorbed in the play, reading certain parts over and over. He even skipped lunch on Saturday because he was so engrossed in the story.

Come Monday, he was eager to share his thoughts with the class.

"Now then," Mr. Hand began. "Who can tell me where the ghost first appears?"

Simon threw his right hand into the air, as high as he could reach without pushing his shoulder out of joint. Apparently, Mr. Hand didn't notice him, and Simon could see that no one else seemed to know the answer.

"Well then," the teacher went on, seeming not to see Simon's flagpole of an arm, "let me put the matter differently. Who is the ghost? That is, who was the ghost when he was alive?"

This time Simon raised his hand so high that he lifted himself slightly out of his chair and wiggled his fingers, trying to draw the teacher's attention. Nothing. Mr. Hand seemed to find Simon invisible. Every time Mr. Hand asked a question about the play, Simon was the only student to raise his hand. It was clear that no one else had read the play or, at least, no one felt confident enough to pose answers to Mr. Hand's questions.

"Look here. Indians are supposed to know all about ghosts. I read about your idiotic Ghost Dance. Tell me, why do you think the ghost appeared before Hamlet and the guards?"

"Why doesn't Prince Hamlet seek revenge right away?"

"What seems to be bothering Ophelia?"

"Anyone? Anyone?" he'd ask each time after raising a question, looking around the classroom, through Simon as if he too were a ghost.

Simon sat erect in his uncomfortable chair, holding his hand up so long that he had to prop it up with his other arm after a while. But the teacher never called on him. After a while, Simon stopped raising his hand.

The impatient teacher was growing angry.

"It's obvious that none of y'all have read any of this play. I should have known that a group of Indians couldn't handle Shakespeare. Just like Nigroes."

He slapped his text of the play on his desk and turned to the chalkboard, angrily writing out the week's assignment.

"I want a three-page essay on *Hamlet* by Friday, proving to me that you've read the play! Write on any subject you want; just be sure you prove to me you've read the whole play."

Simon worked on his essay every night. He quoted lines. He wrote about how he thought Hamlet and other characters felt about things, commenting on the psychology of characters without even knowing what psychology is. He wrote about how he himself sometimes felt worry and distress and uncertainty, just like Hamlet, like Ophelia. He even included a paragraph on why he felt the ghost of Hamlet's father felt betrayal and suffering.

All in all, Simon had never written anything like it before, and he was proud of it. He wound up writing what he considered his very best essay, five-and-a-half pages.

On the following Monday, Mr. Hand shuffled about the classroom returning essays.

"Try harder next time, Lone Fight," the teacher remarked snidely, as he deposited Simon's paper face down on the desk.

Simon had been sure that he would be looking at the first A he had ever earned in It no longer belongs to me. It is yours now. Perhaps it always was. English. Surely this time, he thought, surely this time. Mr. Hand's surly comment struck like a dart at the balloon of Simon's confidence; nevertheless, Simon remained hopeful because Mr. Hand always sounded surly and impatient. He turned the paper over, slowly, hoping for the longed-for A. Even a B+ would be welcome, though a little disappointing. He had worked so hard and learned so much about Shakespeare, about drama, about how a story of another person's problems can ignite understanding of your own. More importantly, he had learned that he had an exciting gift for thinking about and writing about literature, something that only days earlier had never occurred to him about himself.

In that instant, while turning over the face-down paper, Simon relished the irony of the moment. Here was one of the most disliked teachers at Wellington, a self-absorbed, disgruntled, impatient, and surly little man who, as luck would have it, had turned Simon on to a wonderful side of himself that would catapult him to the very front of academic excellence. How strange that an enemy can provide such a blessing. Simon suddenly knew that even if his grade weren't an A, even if a B+ or B, he could still feel proud and build on his new pride.

As Simon flattened the turned-over paper, he saw with a breaking heart the same old squatting D, glaring up at him from the top left corner. No comments, no marks of any sort, accompanied the barren letter grade to indicate why the paper had failed so miserably, what there was about it that was wrong, misplaced, or deficient. There were no comments to suggest why this, his most splendid piece of school work, deserved a grade no better than his worst work, no better than his first essay.

Simon turned to look at Willa's essay. It was all marked up in red ink, like it was bleeding to death. And yet, miraculously, there was an A- scribbled at the top. After class, he asked Noah what he received. Noah's grade was a B, only slightly less than his previous B+, which was not at all comforting. When Noah had looked over Simon's paper and praised it, even offering some slight revisions, he had commented to Simon that his own paper was a disaster, something he had thrown together just to answer an assignment. He had told Simon that he neither liked nor understood anything about the play or about the character of Hamlet.

By his own reckoning, Noah expected a very low grade.

Simon eventually asked nearly all the students in the class about their grades, writing down the various names and scores on a piece of paper to help him figure out the puzzle. At first he couldn't make sense of the grades. They seemed random, unrelated to the quality of the work he associated with each student. Several bad papers and poor students got good grades, and several well-written papers by authors he knew were smart students got bad grades. There was no rhyme or reason to it. But then Simon began to picture each author in his mind. He imagined pretty Willa Spotted Elk with her A and George Joseph with his F.

What was different about them? Simon wondered, chewing on the pink, rubber eraser of his yellow number two pencil. Both were perfectly average students, neither smart nor dull witted.

Maybe girls get good grades and boys get bad grades, he puzzled.

On the other hand, he thought, studying the piece of paper

with all the names and corresponding grades written on it, Noah and some other boys got good marks, and some of the girls got failing grades.

Simon thought about the dilemma all day long. That night, as he puzzled and drifted toward sleep, he thought about *Hamlet*, how Shakespeare used dream-like moments to answer questions. He thought about the play-within-a-play and about the ghost coming toward him on the castle's high ramparts and imagined the sound a ghost would make when talking. At some point Simon was dreaming as much as thinking, and he could see and hear the ghostly, semi-transparent king, in and out of focus, always vague and fleeting, like fog, always ghastly and colorless. And then the phantom spoke, whispering the terrible secret from his thin, white lips. The vaporous king spoke directly, not to Hamlet but to Simon.

"Your skin," said the melancholic, silvery ghost.

Simon awoke. In fact he sat up in his bed. *Your skin.* He understood. More accurately, the color of skin was the degree of Indianness. He turned on the table lamp and retrieved his piece of paper on which he had copied grades and names. Students who were half-breeds or even of lesser Indian blood, Indian but white, received better marks and more praise and attention from Mr. Hand. Noah was a half-breed. Willa one quarter. In fact, every student who earned a high grade was a half-breed. Every student who was a full-blood, Simon included, received a low grade. Simon and George Joseph had the most Indian-looking features in the class. Both had darker skin than anyone else. Even their noses and lips were more Indian looking.

Mr. Hand had a grading system after all. He didn't, as Simon first thought, assign grades randomly, without rhyme or reason. His system was based on appearances. The less Indian-looking the student, the better the grade.

Simon wondered what he should do about his epiphany.

Should he tell the other students? Should he tell the administration? Start a rebellion? Do nothing? Weep?

To be or not to be.

Suddenly, Hamlet's dilemma made more sense than ever to Simon. Should he act or do nothing? He slept on it until the next day. By morning he decided to tell the other students what he had concluded. He didn't mention his dream. He sought out many of his classmates at breakfast, showing them the sheet of paper with each student's name and his or her grade. He told them what he suspected. They all agreed, all except Nila Harjo, who never made less than an A and wasn't about to give up her belief in her perfect record just because she was fair-skinned and blue-eyed.

Little by little, a simple plan was formulated. Each student would write his or her next paper as always. But then each would trade with another student—each Indian-looking full-blood with a less Indian-looking half-breed. They would deceive the teacher by writing under assumed names.

And, sadly, it worked perfectly. The grades followed the names. Students who usually received good grades but who had exchanged names with students who did not failed, and those who normally received F's and D's earned A's and B's under other names. The hypothesis was corroborated. The theory held.

Feeling vindicated, Simon was further encouraged by several class members, who convinced him to carry the results of their concern to the administration. Several students went with him. In all, five students marched into the administration building, energized both by anger and by a sense of pride in their risk and daring to right a wrong, that Mr. Hand would feel the hand of justice. They had to sit in the hall for thirty minutes waiting for the assistant headmaster, who was on an important long-distance phone call. It was his job to deal with academic issues. By the time he finally opened his door, two of the students had already left to attend a class. He invited the three to sit down.

"What's on your mind?" he asked, closing the office door behind him.

He was a stern man, younger than the headmaster by ten years or more.

Simon told him the story. The assistant headmaster listened carefully, taking notes and asking questions. When the meeting was over, he stood up and escorted the three students to the door, shaking their hands on the way out.

"I'm certainly glad you brought this to my attention," he said. "It's quite a serious matter. We'll get it resolved soon, I promise. We can't allow this kind of behavior at Wellington."

Ironically, the man kept his word.

He interviewed Mr. Hand, after which they decided that Simon and the other students had cheated. They were guilty of plagiarism. Everyone received a zero for the assigned paper. No one in that class ever received an A again. For the remainder of his time at Wellington, Mr. Hand would never give another A, regardless of a paper's quality.

Mr. Hand pursued his own version of equality.

"Y'all thought you could fool me," he told the class the day after the failed coup. "But y'all thought wrong. Indians just ain't smart 'nough to fool a white man."

For the rest of the year, Simon cared nothing about literature. His papers were always short of the requirement, poorly organized, full of misspellings, and written at the last moment. He never raised his hand in class, never offered his opinion, never read the book. Instead, he spent the empty hours staring out the window, having become, successfully, what the teacher expected of him.

Chapter Seven

THE DEAD MUST BE LONELY. Every time Elijah High Horse walked past the cemetery of dead Indian children, their tired and miserable ghosts waved at him. During the first weeks he waved back, even smiled awkwardly at them, but the spirits didn't stop there. Because only Elijah could see them, the ghosts walked alongside him, howling unintelligibly, pleading with their hollow eyes for him to stop and listen, trying to grab hold of him with their vaporous hands, wispy as smoke from a dying campfire.

But Elijah had not yet learned to hear the dead.

Now, whenever he had to walk through the place, he tried to ignore them, acting as if he didn't see them milling about aimlessly between headstones, and little by little, week after week, the ghosts began to forget that he had ever seen them at all.

JIMMY RED CLOUD DISAPPEARED eight days before the big, school-wide Halloween party. No one knew what had happened to him. At first, school officials thought he had run away. Runaways were a common feature of the school. But Jimmy's friends weren't buying any of it. Most of his possessions remained in his small room. All of his clothes were neatly folded in dresser drawers. His pocket watch, two framed pictures of his family, and his worn-out wallet containing eight dollars were all still sitting on the dresser top. Most importantly, his portable chess set still lay on his bed. He took that game everywhere—not only to classes but also to the cafeteria. On many nights, he'd sit in the dormitory lobby playing anyone who would play with him. Sometimes he sat by himself playing both sides.

If he had run away, Jimmy's friends argued, he certainly would not have left his wallet and chess set.

Eventually, school officials gave up searching and turned the matter over to the local sheriff's office, which investigated the circumstances of Jimmy's disappearance for two days before announcing that he had run away, despite obvious evidence to the contrary.

About as quickly as the ink dried on the sheriff's official report, so too did the school administration's interest in the matter. That was because nearly everyone imagined he'd appear one day at his family's home. That was the usual pattern. He would then be escorted back to Wellington, back through the wrought-iron gates, back to where he belonged.

But Jimmy started showing up at Elijah's window one night.

That's when Elijah knew Jimmy was dead.

At first Elijah tried to ignore the floating ghost outside his second-floor window, but after the third night the ghost started coming into his room. Elijah pulled the blanket over his head, hoping it would go away. Sometimes, it would disappear in a blink, but more often than not it would hover above his narrow bed, its dark mouth moving, trying to speak. Just as with the big-antlered deer on the sand bar, the sad, lifeless man in the subway, and the restless ghosts in the cemetery, Elijah could only see, not hear, the dead, see Jimmy floating at his window, see him, plaintive, in his room.

At first he didn't tell anyone what he saw, but eventually he told Simon, Noah, and Lucy at breakfast while eating a bowl of sticky oatmeal.

"You know that kid who ran away . . . Jimmy something?" he asked his friends in between bites.

"Red Cloud," Simon replied. "He was in my geography class."

Noah joined in the conversation. "Yeah, I knew him. He was a nice guy. Too bad he ran away. Hope he's okay."

Elijah refilled his milk glass while speaking.

"I don't think he ran away."

"What do you mean?" Lucy asked, her face scrunched up in a puzzled expression.

"I don't think he ran away at all," Elijah repeated quietly, setting down the glass pitcher and looking at his empty bowl, a few flakes of oats stuck to the side.

All three friends stopped eating, urging Elijah to explain.

"I've seen him." Elijah paused before speaking again. "He comes to my room every night."

"Comes to your room?" Noah asked. Elijah had not spoken to his friends about his being a shaman. He was embarrassed and worried what they'd think.

But Simon knew. He remembered the day in the subway in the big city. He remembered how Elijah had seen the dead father of the grease-haired hooligan.

"I mean Jimmy's dead," Elijah said flatly. "His ghost comes to visit me, only I don't want nothin' to do with it."

The three friends listened patiently while Elijah described the ghostly events of the preceding several nights. Noah and Lucy kept glancing at each other, exchanging looks of skepticism. When he was done, Simon recited the bizarre incident in the big city subway. The looks of skepticism turned to wonder. Indeed, Lucy's doubt turned into sympathy for the ghost. She felt sorry for it. For some reason she thought about what the choir teacher might have done if he had caught her the night he tried to fondle Maggie in their dorm room.

She wondered if she had come close to being a ghost.

Eventually, Noah and Simon formulated a plan. That night they would sneak into Elijah's room after curfew and wait with him until the ghost came, which was usually a little before midnight. Lucy couldn't come because there was no easy way to sneak a girl into a boy's dormitory. Elijah would have to tell his roommate, Moses Crow, so that he wouldn't tell on them. Moses was an okay roommate. He was a year younger than Elijah and at least thirty pounds overweight. But Moses kept mostly to himself. He played flute in the school band, and he would sit on the edge of his bed practicing for hours before bedtime. Sometimes his mother sent him homemade cookies, which he generously shared with Elijah.

That night after supper, the boys tried to work on their homework in the common area, eager—for the first time since attending Wellington—for bedtime to arrive. All three were distracted but tried not to show it. When the floor monitors yelled, "Bedtime!" all three boys immediately rose and went to their rooms, closed their doors, and lay awake on their creaking beds, staring at the slow-turning hands of their wall clocks, waiting exactly one hour—time enough for the dorm to settle in for the night—until Noah and Simon would sneak down the hallway to Elijah's room. If asked, they would simply say they were going to the bathroom.

Simon arrived first, knocking softly.

Noah arrived a minute later.

The boys, Moses Crow included, sat in the near dark quietly playing cards until it was near midnight. Moses had placed a small lamp beneath his bed with a towel over it to swallow most of the light. If the floor monitor passed by in the hallway and saw light pouring from under the door, they would all be in trouble. The available light was so weak that each boy had to hold his fan of cards close to his face. Shortly after the two clock hands aligned at the top of their perfect, mechanical orbit, Elijah stopped playing and stood up.

"He's here," he announced calmly, as if he were expecting a guest, as if it were routine to see the dead.

The other boys stopped playing and looked around, seeing

nothing, only the shadowy, dark room and a net of stars, which filled the black sky outside the closed window.

"Where?" asked Moses, following Elijah's gaze.

"Right there, standing by the radiator in front of the window. Can't you see him?"

Both Simon and Noah stood up and walked closer to the window.

"There's nothing here," Noah said, beginning to think this was all a prank.

But Simon knew better. He sat down on Moses' bed and addressed Elijah.

"What's he look like? What's he doing?"

Elijah described what he saw.

"It's Jimmy all right," Elijah whispered. "He's just standing there, looking around, like he lost something."

Moses and Noah stood beside Elijah, trying to see something from his angle. But still, to them, the room looked the same.

As Elijah sat down on the edge of his bed, Noah walked toward the window just as the ghost floated toward Elijah. The ghost of Jimmy Red Cloud passed right through Noah and stopped directly before Elijah and worked its mouth frantically.

"It . . . it's trying to tell me something, I think," Elijah said aloud to his friends.

But the other boys saw nothing, only Elijah sitting on the edge of his narrow bed, looking slightly upward, his eyes intent on something nearby, invisible.

Finally, Elijah spoke directly to the ghost.

"I don't understand you. What do you want?" he asked.

The spirit turned, floated back toward the window, through it, and then hovered outside, two stories high, motioning with one hand to follow. The other arm hung limp at its side, twisted impossibly backward as if broken. After several minutes, the image began to vanish like dissipating fog.

Elijah walked to the window, looking out for a long time before he spoke.

"It's gone," he finally said to the panes of glass before turning around.

The other boys quietly asked all kinds of questions. In the end, however, all were in agreement that the ghost of Jimmy Red Cloud had a real presence and somehow wanted something. He wanted Elijah to follow him somewhere. They sat on the floor, talking for another half hour until each boy crept back to his own room for the night.

Halloween was a couple of days away, the coming Friday. The cafeteria was already partially decorated with dancing skeletons and a variety of small, toothy jack-o'-lanterns fashioned from real pumpkins grown by one of the kitchen workers. Orange napkins on every table included the black silhouette of a witch flying a broomstick. At breakfast, Noah, Simon, and Elijah told Lucy what had happened. As she listened, tiny black hairs on her thin arms raised stiffly.

After listening to everything, Lucy summed up what the others suspected.

"He wants you to go find him," she said. "His body. He wants you to find it."

Everyone was speechless after that. The idea of finding a dead body was fearsome.

Elijah spoke first.

"We'd have to wait until he comes again and follow him."

For the rest of the day, whenever any of the four saw another, they huddled to refine plans for that night. An all-school Halloween party and dance was to be held until after midnight. No one would miss four students in all the excitement. Lucy was to sneak down to that open window on the first floor of her dorm a little before midnight, the same window through which she had escaped the choir teacher. She'd lower herself out the window, hide in the bushes, and wait for a signal. They planned what they would take along: warm jackets against the near-winter cold, flashlights, a pack of matches and a candle, a length of coiled rope, and a bag of cookies in case they got hungry.

Thirty minutes before midnight, Simon and Noah crept into Elijah's room and waited. Moses changed his mind, saying it was too cold outside. He said he'd catch a cold, maybe pneumonia.

When Elijah signaled that the punctual ghost had arrived, the boys hurried out the side door of the dormitory and followed Elijah as he followed the ghost. Noah flicked on his flashlight twice toward Lucy's dorm—their prearranged signal. Lucy ran across the lawn, and all four followed Elijah, who kept the others informed of the spirit's gestures, as it floated through the foggy cemetery teaming with gloomy specters, seen only by Elijah, who tried to brush them away like mosquitoes. Noah, Simon, and Lucy tried not to imagine what their friend was seeing.

Once past the iron-and-red-brick gate, the ghost swept across the paved road and across a fallow field on the other side, its one arm dangling uselessly. An owl's hoot echoed softly from the far tree line, and a fingernail of moon hung on the edge of the earth above an old, partially collapsed barn.

The night was spooky and dark and cold. Lucy stayed close to Noah, who had picked up a thick walking stick somewhere along the way. For almost a mile the band of friends followed Elijah as the phantom led them into the dark woods beyond the field, frequently turning and beckoning Elijah to follow. After a while, the ghost grew increasingly excited, quickening its floating pace through the darkness. It seemed eager.

Following became more and more difficult, as the four friends picked their way among the bramble of sapling, over dead falls, and through patches of thorny brush—all of which the ghost of Jimmy Red Cloud passed through without concern.

Suddenly, the anxious band of friends emerged at a clearing in the woods. At the center was a large mound of ash and partially burned logs—the cold, gray remains of a great fire. The brittle, brown grass all around was trampled, as if crushed beneath a hundred angry feet.

Beneath a trickle of moonlight falling through the clouds, the ghost of Jimmy Red Cloud stopped abruptly on the edge of the clearing, as abruptly as the apparition had first appeared outside Elijah's window. Elijah waited for something to happen, but nothing happened. The ghost just stood in the clearing, in the moonlight, in the cold, wet silence of the late October night. Then, growing indistinct in its features, it slowly moved away from the clearing and to the edge of the surrounding woods, hovering momentarily before fading, until it vanished altogether.

Elijah didn't know what to say or do. He felt a little embarrassed. No one knew what to do. Why had the spirit brought them so far if only to leave them in this unlikely place?

Finally, Lucy spoke.

"Maybe what he wants us to find is right around here."

Staying within sight of one another, the four split apart, looking for something, anything, though unable to name what it might be. They methodically searched in a wide circle around the spot where the ghost had paused before moving away. They found nothing on the field. Cautiously, they pushed into the edge of dense forest surrounding the clearing, just beyond where Elijah had last seen the vaporous image. The clouds thickened and grew darker, making more and more difficult the task of seeing the ground clearly.

Only Elijah and Simon had flashlights.

Suddenly, Simon yelled that he had found something.

The three friends scrambled through the undergrowth to where he stood, peering down at and into a sizable hole in the ground. Both Elijah and Simon shone their lights down the hole. It was an old mine shaft. The countryside was full of them—old, forgotten, and frequently unmarked and exposed pits left after the exploration for coal. The opening measured only about four feet across, maybe a bit larger. The flanks of the hole were grown over with vegetation. With both flashlights focused on the bottom, they could see something faintly illuminated in the dark.

It was a body.

And although it was face down, with one arm projecting awkwardly from beneath, they knew it was the body of Jimmy Red Cloud.

They tied the rope they had brought to a nearby tree, and Elijah lowered himself into the pit, while Simon, Lucy, and Noah peered over the edge, Simon training the yellowish beam of his flashlight on Elijah's descent. Once down, Elijah reached out to the neck of the body to check for a pulse, just in case the boy was not dead. The instant he touched the body, Elijah saw Jimmy's death. He saw it as clearly as though it were springing fresh from his own memory.

Elijah saw the boy dancing on the field around a great bonfire, at night, surrounded by other Indian boys and girls from the school. He recognized several of the faces. Most of them were older, juniors and seniors. They were dancing Indian-style, just as they had danced back home, back wherever they had come from. Several boys sat on a log beating homemade drums and singing, their smiling brown faces lit by firelight.

Elijah had heard about this place, but he thought it just a rumor. Sometimes, he overheard older kids talking about going to "the dancing place" in the woods to dance at night. The place was far enough away so that they would not be caught. It had to be done in secret because Indian-style dancing, like speaking their native language, was prohibited at the school. According to the rumors, students at Wellington had been coming to this place ever since the school first opened. It was an underground movement, an act of defiance, one of the reasons their culture was never fully stripped from many of the children at Wellington.

In the vision, Elijah saw Jimmy wipe sweat from his forehead and walk off into the edge of the woods alone. He was cooling down from the strenuousness of dancing when he inadvertently fell into the hole nearly covered by overgrowth. Elijah saw the boy falling, smacking the earth littered with rocks, which had worked loose over the years from the shaft's walls and tumbled to the bottom. He saw Jimmy lying there, crumpled in a broken heap, his one arm twisted backward, blood trickling into his eyes.

And then the vision went black, and he knew that Jimmy had died alone, frightened he would never be found.

That was why his spirit sought Elijah.

Elijah climbed out from the musty-smelling hole and described to his friends what he had seen, while a thin, ghost-like layer of fog rolled lazily over the ground, glowing eerily in patches of moonlight.

The friends talked about what they should do. If they told school officials where to find the body, they would surely discover the field of secret dancing and shut it down forever. On the other hand, the ghost of Jimmy Red Cloud made it clear that it wanted its body found.

It wasn't simply a matter of right and wrong. The situation was more complicated than that.

On the way back to the school, Elijah decided that he would tell some of the older students that he and his friends had stumbled upon the body. He couldn't tell them about his visions. They'd just think he was weird, and they probably wouldn't believe him anyway.

The next day Elijah tracked down five of the older boys he had seen in the vision and told them about Jimmy's body. He gave them a crude map, indicating the location of the pit relative to the dancing field. That night, under cover of darkness, the boys slipped out of their dorms, crossed the asphalt road and the wide, fallow field, making their way to the secret dancing place. From there, they used Elijah's map to find the body, which they managed to lift from the hole using the rope Elijah assured them was securely tied to a nearby tree. They laid the body on a stretcher made of a heavy dorm-room blanket tied between two long poles.

The boys took turns carrying the stretcher, two at a time.

When they returned to the school, the impromptu pall bearers passed quietly through the rusted, iron gates and leaned the stiff body against a headstone in the cemetery of dead Indian children, close to the sidewalk so that that school officials would find him in the morning.

Just as the older boys had predicted, there was no investigation, no sounding of alarm. There was only the brief ceremony and the burial to come. Such events happened.

Elijah saw the ghost for the last time that night. It stood beside his bed, looking down at him, smiling as it faded into a memory. He didn't have to say a single word.

Two days later, Jimmy Red Cloud's body was buried in the school's cemetery, adding his name to the hundreds of Indian names already carved into headstones. All of his friends, Noah, Simon, Lucy, and Elijah included, stood in a close circle, singing hymns, as the simple pine casket was lowered into the ground.

When the memorial service was over, a lone grounds-keeper filled the grave with shovels full of earth, as the first snowflakes of winter began to fall, cold and silent as the remorseless cemetery.

Chapter Eight

NOVEMBER WAS ALWAYS a hard month at Wellington. The thin, white blanket of snow did nothing to hide the harshly institutional outlines of the school. If anything, it somehow made the institution look more colorless, more black and white, with intermediate shades of gray, as if the place were empty of life. The ground was gray, the roofs were gray, the barren shrubs and naked trees looked black or gray or some lifeless shade between, and the gray-black smoke billowing from the chimneys and smoke stacks was the only movement on the bleak, wintry scene.

Even the sky seemed steel-like and gloomy.

It was a sad and depressing time for many of the recently arrived children, who, traditionally at this time of the year, experienced their most intense bouts of homesickness. Only during the Christmas season would the gnawing pain be worse. It was the lonely month of abandonment when even the sports fields were forsaken—the football and baseball uniforms and equipment put away for the season, the track field and basketball courts buried under a thin mantle of crusted snow and ice. What little hope and happiness had risen from—or survived—this new life, for whatever reason, seemed to have deserted the brooding dorms and classrooms, the gray woods and sky.

Simon Lone Fight was homesick. He came from a reservation in the Four Corners region, that wide-ranging expanse of the

American Southwest long the domain of the Navajo, the Zuni, the Hopi, and other Indian peoples. And what Simon missed the most, besides his dead mother and father, were his bent-over grandparents, his dog, and hearing the increasingly distant sounds of his Indian language spoken around the house, in the stores and gas stations, at the bingo hall, all over the reservation. Those sounds, coming from the throats of his family, the mouths of relatives, or the lips of perfect strangers, were part of him. The words tumbled inside his heart, ran the winding course of his veins. Unlike many of the students at Wellington, Simon still spoke his language, heard it clearly in his dreams of rocky, red canyons and soaring eagles, of cool, shadowy caves in steep cliff sides.

He had met some other students who were Navajo, though none of them were from his reservation. Sometimes, they would sit together whispering in Navajo, careful not to let teachers overhear them. If caught, younger children had their mouths washed out with lye soap, or were forced to lick the floor, or were paddled and sent to their dorm room without supper—sometimes a combination, sometimes all of the above.

The punishment for older students was of a different order. There were rumors of having needles pushed through tongues as discipline.

One morning at breakfast, Lucy shared a story she had heard from a girl her age, named Ada Lame Deer, whose room was across the hall from Lucy and Maggie.

"Ada told me about a girl named Franny, who graduated last year but who used to room with Ada. Franny once told Ada that early one morning while she was taking a shower, she was caught singing a song her grandmother had taught her. The song was full of Indian words with the names of animals. While she was in the shower, the water suddenly went off. When she rubbed the soap from her eyes and looked, the dorm matron was standing there, right in the shower stall."

Simon stopped eating his cold scrambled eggs.

"Holy cow!" he said. "Right there in the shower?"

Lucy nodded and then continued her story.

"The old lady told Franny that she would have to come to her office as soon as she got dressed. When Franny went into her office, the matron closed the door and began lecturing her on how wrong it is to speak or even sing Indian words. Then she opened a drawer in her desk and pulled out a small, flat box and opened the lid. She showed the box to Franny and asked, 'Do you know what these are?' Inside the box were about half a dozen hat pins, each with a little black ball attached at one end. Franny knew what they were. Ada told me that Franny had nightmares about the pins and that she was afraid to sing anymore after that."

The school's long and clouded history included persistent stories—perhaps rumor, perhaps recollection—of punishment even more severe, meted out for the crime of speaking a Native language, punishment that had resulted in the accidental deaths of several children, their bodies, like Jimmy Red Cloud, deposited in hastily dug graves in the cemetery, the records of their deaths falsified.

But the Indian-speaking students found one another nonetheless. And like those students who stayed connected to their tribal traditions by dancing at the secret place in the forest, they found places to gather in secret where they could once again hear the beautiful, ancient words of home, despite the many posted signs and lectures warning them to speak only English.

After his demoralizing encounter with Mr. Hand, Simon began noticing that many of the school staff, easily half or more, were immigrants or at least descendants of immigrants, like Mr. Weil. Most spoke with strange accents. Simon was right. Many of the staff, or their parents or grandparents, had come from Poland or Germany or Sweden, from Italy or Hungary, from Korea or China or Japan, from Mexico or unfamiliar countries in Africa. Simon had heard some of the kitchen workers singing songs in their parents' language, but none of them was ever punished, as far as Simon could tell, for speaking in any language other than English, or, apparently, for clinging to old ways.

Indians, whose forebears had lived on this land for ten thousand years, were punished for speaking a single word of their language, and yet, Simon was taking Latin. He hated it. The classroom walls were adorned with posters of Latin root words, and yet, right above the teacher's desk hovered one of the ubiquitous "English Only" posters.

Occasionally, Simon shared his observations and his mounting concern over this issue, mostly with Noah and Elijah, but sometimes with other classmates. No one, not even those who secretly spoke in their Native language, seemed willing to talk about the subject and most seemed a little offended that Simon would bring it up. It was one thing to hang on to a few words and to share them in secret, but it was quite another to complain about "the problem" in a more general sense. Noah even warned Simon once, "You gotta keep that stuff to yourself, Simon. You could get us all in into trouble." So, Simon didn't talk.

Simon brooded.

He seldom paid attention any more in English class. What was the use? But he took a dark interest in geography. Whenever he had the chance to check out a library book, it was always about geography. He was interested in place names, the names of rivers and creeks; of the origins of the names of states. Simon made A's on his geography tests. He soon learned the state capitols, all of them. He was the only one in class who could immediately distinguish between the capitols of North and South Dakota, the only one who could correctly spell Connecticut, the only one who could name all eight states bordering Tennessee.

And yet Simon brooded.

On the one hand, the nation sought to eliminate Indians,

moving them every time the land-hungry nation needed more land. Still, the new nation wanted a sense of connection to the land, something that made the land-stealers feel as though they had been part of the continent since the beginning, almost mythic. So they kept the Indian names for everything—for rivers and creeks and lakes and even towns and states. Indian names litter the maps: Massachusetts, Mississippi, Connecticut, Utah, Talladega, Tallahassee, Tuscaloosa, Seattle, Milwaukee . . . there are thousands of such names.

One day after lunch, while waiting for gym class, Simon was sitting on a bleacher in the gymnasium and quietly speaking in Navajo to George Pancake, both boys from time to time nervously looking over their shoulder, unaware that the gym teacher, Mr. Koprowski, a second generation Polish-American who still spoke Polish to his grandmother at home, had been watching them from afar, suspicious of their actions.

Koprowski's demeanor toward the Indian children was difficult for the students to understand. In many ways he was an admirable role model—tall, muscular, athletic, full of commanding self-confidence—everything a young boy wants to be. Even the female teachers and staff seemed attracted to him.

"Boys are men in progress," he often said, a kind of tin slogan.

And most of the boys appreciated the premise. Nevertheless, Koprowski was, in their minds, mean. Not tough. Mean. When a boy couldn't climb the rope or do enough pull-ups, Koprowski belittled him until the boy lost all self-respect, until some of the younger boys who couldn't perform properly broke down and cried, until some of them threw up the next time they even looked at a rope or a high bar.

Mr. Koprowski crept beneath the bleachers, quietly making his way through the framework until he hunched directly beneath Simon and George, where he could hear Simon talking to his friend in Navajo.

Both boys were as happy to speak their language as they were frightened of being caught. They loved to hear the words spoken, every syllable a reminder of home. In the guttural sounds they could feel the blazing sun, see wary jackrabbits emerge in the night, and smell the red desert after rain.

In their enthusiasm, neither of the boys noticed the gym teacher beneath their feet or saw him crawl out the far side and climb onto the bleacher, bounding two steps at a time, up toward them.

Mr. Koprowski grabbed Simon by the arm, yanked him to his feet, and dragged him down the steps, across the polished hardwood floor, and down the hallway to his office, where he called the headmaster, Dr. Dichter, the son of a German immigrant who still spoke German among his family, despite the fact that his country of heritage had twice waged a war against all of Europe, dragging America and her sons into both conflicts.

The students and some of the school staff had an obvious nickname for him.

Dr. Dickhead.

Five minutes later, Simon and the gym teacher were both standing in the headmaster's office, the terrified Simon apologizing profusely, the headmaster yelling, spitting as he screamed, pounding a fist on his desk, knocking over a cup full of yellow pencils, each sharpened precisely to the same dark point.

"I caught him red handed," the gym teacher said, proudly, as though he were describing how he stalked and shot a deer. "I heard him loud and clear. Didn't I, Shrimp?" he said, leaning close to Simon's face, his breath rancid like soured milk.

Simon tried to apologize.

"I'm sorry, really. I just forgot. I won't do it again, honest. I just forgot."

Dr. Dichter came around the desk with a wooden paddle in his hand. Mr. Koprowski grabbed Simon and bent him over the desk, holding pressure on his neck and arms so that he couldn't move.

"We're not fools, Lone Flight," the headmaster mispronounced Simon's name as he yelled and smacked the paddle against Simon's behind. "You think we're stupid, that we don't know what you're doing. You Indians think you can hoodwink us into believing that you've forgotten your language, but we know better."

He beat the boy between sentences, pausing only long enough to take a deep breath amid strokes.

Simon held back his tears, held back his screams. He closed his eyes and imagined running through canyons, the sun hot on his neck, his dog at his side.

"You think you don't have to listen to us, but you will. You think you can outlast us, but you won't." With that the headmaster finished beating the boy, set down the paddle, and wiped away sweat running down his temple.

Dr. Dichter pulled out a Bible from a drawer and dropped it heavily on the desk top.

"You see this?" he said, pointing to the thick, black book. "If English is good enough for the Bible, it's good enough for America and good enough for you."

Simon knew better. He resisted as best he could beneath the force of Dichter's sarcasm. He stared at the dense, gold-leafed book, his eyes welling up with tears.

Dr. Dichter reached into the same drawer and retrieved a ring of keys, maybe twenty or more. He looked hard at the boy before he spoke to the gym teacher.

"Bring him along. I know how to break him," he said, his voice hard and flat. "We'll make an example of him."

Mr. Koprowski seized Simon's thin arm, bent it behind his back, and pushed him through the office door.

The angry men led Simon out of the administration building and across the school grounds toward an old maintenance building, while hundreds of Indian eyes watched from classroom windows. All the older students knew what was happening. The same scene had unfolded hundreds of times in the preceding seventy years. The helpless spectators knew what awaited Simon inside the building.

Some of the girls wept.

Some of the boys looked away.

But inside each of them—every last one—resentment smoldered like white smoke from a burning sage bundle.

Simon had heard the stories and feared what lay on the other side of the chained door. He shuddered while the headmaster struggled to open the padlock and pull the clanking chain through the welded brackets.

Fear rose in the boy, diluting his resolve. He wanted to be strong. He had not cried when they beat him, and he tried to keep his silence now. But the fear and uncertainty broke him.

"Please! Please don't leave me here!" he begged, trying to wriggle free. "Let me go back. I'll do better. I promise not to speak Navajo again. I swear."

When he heard his own words, Simon felt his heart break. He opened his mouth to retract the words, but nothing came out, and the sorrowful words did not return.

The headmaster looked around him; saw the many faces in windows and doorways, the watchful eyes.

"You need to be taught a lesson, Lone Flight. There will be no Indian spoken at Wellington!" he said loud enough to be heard by some of the nearby spectators.

The men pushed Simon through the door and into the large room, lit only by a bank of small windows, up high near the ceiling, which let some natural light filter into the dusty, mildew-coated room. The building was heated by an old, industrial radiator, which knocked and rattled as if a small animal were caged inside it. Nowadays, the building was used mostly to store summer equipment: lawn mowers, fertilizer and grass-seed broadcasters, rakes, shovels, wheel barrows. An array of tools—large and small—were scattered on work benches or suspended on hooks to the walls. Several cement blocks were stacked on the floor. And although the room was moderately heated, Simon trembled as he apologized, promising never to speak his language again.

"I'm sorry! I'm sorry!" Simon pleaded, finally crying, his knees weakening.

But the men did not seem to hear him. Instead, they led him toward the back of the musty-smelling room toward two horizontal rows of rusted-metal water pipes running the length of the outside wall, about three feet above the concrete floor. About every eight feet or so, a vertical brace anchored the pipes to the wall. The gym teacher handcuffed Simon's hand to the lower pipe, between the corner and the first bracket, and yanked it hard to test it.

"That outta keep him. He ain't goin' nowhere," he said to his boss, his voice dry as a biscuit. Then he bent close to Simon's face, his obstinate nose almost touching Simon's.

"Be seein' ya, Shrimp," he sneered.

Before leaving, the headmaster walked over to a rusty spigot and partially filled a galvanized pail with water, which he handed to Simon.

"Two days," he said sharply.

That's all he said before closing the heavy metal door, leaving Simon in the dingy, stale-air room.

Simon stood looking at his new surroundings, trying to pull his thin wrist free. But the handcuffs were too tight, biting deeper into his skin the harder he pulled. Outside, he could hear the men pull the heavy, rusted chain through the welded door and snap the lock. Simon had heard about this place. Unused tools weren't the only thing they imprisoned here. The building also served as a prison of sorts for Indians who broke the most important rule of the school.

English Only!

There was nothing to make Simon's incarceration comfortable—no mattress or blankets, no stool or chair—only the unyielding concrete floor, the bad-tempered radiator, and the downward curve of rusted metal pipes as they approached the corner and pierced the wall, allowing the thin boy the luxury of lying down in the corner without having to overextend his arms upward. In the other direction, he could slide the handcuffs along the pipe for about eight feet, until the supporting bracket stopped him.

Eight feet.

The length of a jail cell.

Spider webs hung densely in several corners and crowded areas of the room, draped between large pieces of equipment. Black widows. Brown recluses. The room was perfect for them—warm, dark, and quiet as a tomb. Simon shuddered. In the past, some students had almost died from spider bites, untreated during their imprisonment, undiscovered until the door finally opened. And one time, so the story goes, a girl had been locked in the building one winter. That night the radiator stopped working, and the girl was found dead when they opened the doors two days later, her body cold as the brick walls, frozen as the water pipes.

A curious mouse peeked out from behind a pile of fertilizer bags and then scurried across the floor, squeezing through the narrow space between the bottom of the door and the concrete slab, leaving Simon alone again.

Simon slid along the piping to an empty bucket, its walls and bottom crusted black—a honey bucket for going to the bathroom. And although the sight and smell of the bucket disgusted him, Simon had to go.

Afterward, he experimented, trying to learn how best to sit or lie down. He could sit with his back to the wall with his arm suspended over his head, but the arm quickly lost circulation, and he'd have to stand up again. Lying down was not much better, but if he moved into the dark and filthy corner, his shackled arm could reside nearly level with his reclining body. As the sun set, Simon's stomach growled the way his dog sometimes growled at snakes or scorpions.

He was already hungry.

At first, the musty quiet was peaceful. Simon had felt relieved that the men were gone. No more paddling. No more sermons. No more smelling Mr. Koprowski's bad breath, and no more of the headmaster's sarcasm. But then the loneliness and nausea began to creep in on him. Simon began to see himself as if from a removed viewpoint. He saw a handcuffed little boy. He saw a weakling who cried and tried to apologize. He saw a frightened kid who didn't know how to live like this. And although he fought to control the panic, Simon knew that this kind of isolation could kill the spirit. For the first time in his life—including even that horrible moment when he learned that his parents had died—Simon felt that wave of despair that unhinges a human being from all hope.

He wondered how he would last for two days.

And just at that moment, on that dreadful edge, Simon heard a scraping sound. It came from the corner of the room, where the pipes descended through the back wall just behind him. He cocked his head, following the sound, sliding his handcuffs along the piping. Near the corner, about waist high, he saw one of the bricks in the wall jiggling, then slide out of its place altogether, toward the outside. And then came the slant light of late evening, crowded through the square opening, gray-white and fragile like porcelain.

Simon bent over and peered through the hole.

He could see Noah and George Pancake, who had attended the school for two years. George knew everything about Wellington, including its dirty secrets. He knew about the brick, how the mortar had long ago been scratched away when teachers first began to use the building as a prison. Like the dancing field, it was something the school officials knew nothing about. George had been handcuffed to the pipes on three separate occasions during his first year, once for three days.

"Thought you might be hungry," George whispered, leaning close to the opening, shoving a cold fried chicken leg and two biscuits through the hole in the wall.

Then Noah leaned close. "Don't worry, Simon," he said, smiling. "Everyone will help you."

And they did.

All day long, at varying times, students, both boys and girls, took turns sneaking to the back of the building, creeping through the bushes along the wall, and pulling out the brick. They comforted Simon with conversation, pushed bits of food through the hole, and passed encouraging notes from other students. They were even able to pass him a thin blanket through the gap, feeding it a bit at a time, wound up like a rope. And although it was difficult to sleep on the hard floor with one hand cuffed to the pipes, it became a bearable prison.

Naturally, his closest friends—Lucy, Elijah, and Noah—visited him the most. It seemed as though one of them was always with him during the long days.

This is the way it had always been done. The teachers laid down the rules, and the students broke them. The school tried to eradicate their language, tried to beat it out of them, tried to torture it out of existence with suffering, but the students always found ways to fight back as best they could.

Noah came for the blanket before Headmaster Dichter returned to set Simon free. They had to hide all evidence of assistance. When the man opened the door at the end of the second day, he expected to find the boy crying in the darkness, whimpering, pleading to be released.

"Are you ready to go back to your room?" he sternly asked.

Simon nodded.

"Did you learn your lesson?"

Simon nodded again.

"Are you going to speak that Indian gobbledygook in my school again?" the balding man asked, fishing out the handcuff key from his vest pocket.

Simon looked straight into the headmaster's eyes before he answered.

"No sir. I promise," he said.

In Navajo.

In a fit, Dichter stormed out of the building, screaming so loud that students, who had gathered on the sidewalks, in windows, or congregated in doorways heard him.

"Two more days!" he yelled, as he slammed the metal door and fumbled with the chain and lock.

The next two days were just as uncomfortable but less terrifying than the first. Moses Crow even came to sit outside the brick wall, shivering in the cold. He brought Jimmy Red Cloud's portable chess set, and he'd play Simon, who could only see the pieces when Moses carefully lifted the game to the height of the rectangular opening.

"Move my knight next to your pawn by your queen," Simon would say, squatting to peer through the hole. "No, on the other side."

But their games never lasted long because Moses always got too cold.

One boy brought a deck of cards and he and Simon played poker, Simon pushing his discards through the peek-hole.

"Gimme three," he'd say.

Three new cards were pushed through.

"Full house!" exclaimed Simon, showing his winning hand.

But more than anything, Simon was happy for all the girls that came to visit. They'd ask how he was doing, and some even asked him to teach them Navajo. In between classes, and whenever the girls had free time, they'd sneak to the back of the building and he'd teach them basic words: hand, face, eyes, yes, no, water, friendship, freedom. In return, they brought him cookies, which they had baked in home economics class.

Simon shared the crumbs with the tiny mouse, his cell mate, which had become so accustomed to him that it sat in the palm of his hand while nibbling its sweet meal, spinning the crumbs in its nimble fingers, its small and black eyes fixed on the boy's smiling face.

Each day was more or less the same. Simon slept uncomfortably, ate when his friends brought food, used the honey bucket, talked to visitors, and played chess or cards. And so it went. Every time the headmaster came to release him, Simon rebelled by continuing to speak Navajo. Every day he strengthened his resolve to keep that one part of him unbroken.

Every day the headmaster's frustration hardened.

Some of the teachers and staff began to feel uncomfortable, whispering among themselves in the halls and empty classrooms.

A thing can be taken too far.

The headmaster was becoming exasperated. To him, his struggle with Simon was a battle he had to win. He couldn't have his staff going against him, questioning his decisions. That might lead to dissidence. He had worked far too hard to build his reputation, for good and for bad. He needed their respect, even their fear. He required a resounding victory in his private Indian war.

Late at night, when no one could see, the headmaster paid Simon a visit.

The sound of the chains being pulled through the door handles woke Simon from his uncomfortable sleep. He sat up, wondering who was coming in the middle of night and to what purpose. Maybe someone had come to release him or to break him out. But then he had the unsettling notion that whoever it was might be coming to kill him, drag him out and bury him in the cemetery in the dead of night, tell folks that he had escaped and run away. *Problem solved.*

The metal door opened, and a shadow loomed in the doorway, stars outlining the dark form. Then the door closed with a clank and the room was pitch black again.

The ominous shadow was inside the room.

"Hello? Who's there?" Simon whispered, pressing himself against the brick wall, trying to become part of the wall.

No reply came.

Simon listened for movement where he had seen the shadowy form in the doorway.

He heard nothing.

"Hello?" Simon nervously questioned the darkness, his mouth dry.

Then he heard a rustling followed by what sounded like a match being struck against a matchbox. Twice he heard the familiar sound, and twice the match failed to ignite. On the third try the match lit, and Simon saw the scowling face of the headmaster, twisted and frightening in the flaring light.

Dr. Dichter pulled a candle stub from his trouser pocket and lit the short wick. He sat the burning candle on a stack of cinder blocks and approached the terrified boy.

"I need to end this," said the headmaster, wringing his hands and looking about the dingy, shadowy room as if checking for witnesses. "It's gone on long enough."

Simon tensed, preparing himself for the fierce life or death struggle to come.

But instead of attacking, the headmaster crouched before Simon.

"I'm sure we can come to some mutual agreement, a compromise," said Dichter in an ingratiating tone.

Simon perked up at the thought of being freed. He relaxed his tensed muscles a little.

"You see, Lone Fight, I need your help. Wellington is a big

school. It's impossible for me to know what's going on all the time."

Simon appreciated that the headmaster had pronounced his name properly for the first time.

"I need someone on the *inside*, someone I can trust, who can help me to make the school run better . . . for everyone's sake."

Dichter's tone was pleading, almost piteous.

"I need *your* help."

"How can I . . . help?" asked Simon.

"You could be a secret agent, like in the movies . . . tell me which students are speaking Indian or otherwise breaking the rules. You see, Simon, rules are important, even necessary. They are the glue that holds society together. Otherwise, you have chaos. You can understand that, can't you?"

Simon didn't reply.

"I want to make a deal with you," Dichter continued in the entreating voice. "If you'll help me, be my spy, I'll give you your own room. You won't have to share it with anyone. I'll make sure it even has a radio so you can listen to baseball games. And you can sleep in thirty minutes longer than other students."

"Get my own room, huh? A radio?"

Like every teenage boy, Indian or otherwise, Simon was keen on the idea of having his own radio to listen to ball games. Imagine how popular he would be with the other boys.

"All yours," replied the headmaster, pleased that Simon seemed to be considering his offer.

"And I can sleep in every day?"

"Every day," mirrored Dichter.

"It sure is tempting. And all I gotta do is tell you when other students are breaking the rules?"

"That's it. So what do you say? Can you help me out, Simon? Will you help out your school?"

More than anything else, the last two words hung in the dimness, as if painted on the dark walls with sunlight.

129

Your school.

"I want you to think about it. I'll come back in two days for your answer. Think on it," he warned, picking up the gray pail of drinking water and moving it out of Simon's reach. "Things could always get worse for you."

Dichter extinguished the candle and opened the squeaking metal door.

"Think about this too," said the star-traced shadow standing in the doorway, "Your friends could suffer for your arrogance."

The headmaster closed the door, pulled the clanking chains through the handles, and closed the lock, a now familiar sound to Simon. Simon was unable to return to his uncomfortable sleep. The headmaster's last words wouldn't let him rest.

The next day, Simon told Lucy, Noah, and Elijah about the headmaster's "deal" through the secret peek-hole. He also told them how the headmaster had threatened to punish *them* if he didn't stop resisting and making him look like a fool. Most importantly, Simon told them how Dichter had moved his only source of water, without which he could die.

"What a dickhead!" exclaimed Noah.

Lucy and Elijah shook their heads in disbelief.

"How the hell did he ever get to be in charge of this place?" asked Elijah.

But all four knew that he was made headmaster *because* of such actions.

To combat the headmaster's wicked plan, all three friends brought water to Simon throughout the day. They also told every classmate about the headmaster's offer to make Simon into his spy. At mealtime, notes were passed between tables. By bedtime, every student at Wellington knew.

TWO NIGHTS AFTER the midnight visit, true to his word, the headmaster returned for Simon's answer. If he was anything,

Dichter was punctual. Again Simon heard the rattling chains; again he heard the creaking door open; and again he saw the headmaster's fat, pink face illuminated eerily by match light.

Before saying a word, Dichter looked to make sure the water pail was untouched.

"So, Simon," he said. "How are you holding up? Thirsty, I imagine?"

"I'm okay," replied Simon.

"You must be starving?" he said pulling a sandwich from a brown paper bag. "Bet you'd like a nice ham and cheese sandwich? Made it myself."

"No thanks. I'm not hungry," replied Simon, yawning.

Simon could see that his nonchalant answers and lack of eagerness were infuriating the headmaster, who shoved the sandwich back into the bag.

"Are you prepared to accept my more than generous offer?"

"I think I'll stay here," replied Simon. "I like it here."

Dichter exploded in anger. He kicked the water pail across the cement floor and hurled the brown paper bag against a far wall.

"You can stay here and rot for all I care!" he yelled, spitting out the words, his face as red as a brick wall.

"Two more days!" he shrieked as he opened the door to leave. "No one's ever lasted that long."

ON THE SEVENTH DAY Noah and Lucy brought Simon his mail, a letter from his grandmother. They slid it through the rectangular opening and waited while Simon read it to himself.

"What does it say?" asked Lucy when Simon was finished.

Simon read it aloud to his friends. The letter said that Simon's grandfather had died. Simon was silent for long moments. Lucy and Noah knew that their friend was crying. They remembered that his parents were also dead. But then Simon would clear his throat and read again. When he finished, Simon carefully folded the letter, replaced it inside its envelope, and slid it into his shirt.

On the twelfth day, the headmaster received an anonymous letter that someone had slid under his office door the night before. The typed letter purported to be from a teacher and threatened to call the authorities if Simon wasn't released immediately. Nothing about the letter indicated who might have written it. The letter could have been typed on any of the school's many typewriters. There were thirty of them in Mr. McDuff's typing class.

Frustrated that he could not break the obstinate boy, that he could not wrench the stubborn words from him without killing him, and concerned about a police investigation, Dr. Dichter finally set Simon free. By then, Simon's defiance had become mythic. The story of Lone Fight would be told and retold, whispered like a prayer through the echoing halls of the school for the rest of its existence. Over the years, his name would change, the duration of his imprisonment would vary, the year it happened would be lost, but the myth would endure as all great stories of courage endure.

Chapter Nine

WELLINGTON WASN'T THE BEST PLACE to spend Christmas. The holiday season reminded the children of how much they missed their families. Consequently, the number of students who ran away from school increased considerably as Christmas drew closer. It was a curious and remarkable phenomenon. Dr. Dichter—a man of steadfast habit and predictability, in spite of all appearances, including his ink-black-dyed comb-over to the one side or the other of his broad and usually sweaty head—could track with near precision the December date by the number of runaways, or attempted runaways, reported to him by his staff on a daily basis.

This year would prove no exception.

Two weeks before Christmas, twenty-four Indian children were known to have plotted running away from school. By the next week, the number had nearly doubled. However, by the last few days before Christmas, only a total of twelve students had, indeed, run away. Remarkably, all twelve had been caught and returned and properly punished, their penance painstakingly planned for the rest of the year.

All, that is, except for fifteen year old Lester Black Feather from Oklahoma who had run away and been caught five times in the past two years. Punishing Lester didn't seem to work; he took his punishment in stride. Instead, the headmaster took to punishing Lester's younger sister, Anna. Two years younger than Lester, Anna was locked in her room for three days and paddled twice each day, while her disobedient brother was forced to watch. If he looked away, extra paddles were added. The message was clear to every student with a sibling at the school—and there were many: *Run away and your brother or sister pays the price.*

Punishment of siblings had long been an effective means of control at Wellington. Lester was never the same afterward. For the rest of the school year, he neither spoke openly to anyone nor smiled nor cried. Something inside him ran away for good.

Some say it was pride.

Some say it was hope.

On a dark night during the next year Lester took his own life. The school's cemetery, old and patient, opened its earthen arms and grinned its teeth of headstones.

NOAH BOYSCOUT wanted to run away, just as he wanted to run away from the wolves back home. He was determined not to spend Christmas at Wellington, only this time he had no rabbits to throw to save himself. He stood staring out his dormitory window all morning, wondering how such a small place—and Wellington really was a small place, only a few dozen acres in all—could be filled with so much sorrow, how so many tears could fall from such a small sky.

But it was dangerous to run away in winter. Noah had heard many terrible stories about Indians who ran away. One of them haunted his dreams. It was a sad and tragic story of four boys who had tried to escape toward home during one particularly harsh winter. The tale was now more legend than fact, its sorrowful telling part of the mortar binding the bricks of the school, and it frightened Noah.

Just after the turn of the century, several teenage boys from a Blackfeet reservation in Montana ran away six days before Christmas. All had been on the track team. One even held the school record for the mile. That week, the hardest blizzard ever to hit the east settled in for the long haul. The winds raged and temperatures plummeted so low that farm animals froze to death in their barns, ponds froze to the bottom, families were imprisoned in their homes, and the ceaseless snows shut down all commerce.

Even the moth-like stars shivered.

Nothing moved across the suffering land save a small group of young Indian boys trudging through dense forests, pressing across unyielding fields toward home, slowed by trepidation and snowdrifts and frostbite.

They were found in a small mining town so near death that all the boys had to have their feet amputated. After months in painful convalescence, they were returned to Wellington, where all of them spent their final years at the school in wheel chairs, running foot races only in their dreams.

Other tragic accounts had circulated around the school, year after decade—some less, some more terrible—like the story of what happened to little Molly Fury, who ran away on Christmas Eve night to find her mother. Molly was so young and so small and it was so dark that she didn't get far. A search party was sent out on Christmas Day, and they found her a mere three miles away, frozen through and through at the edge of a backcountry road. For many years, students told of seeing her blue-fleshed ghost wandering the school grounds, bits of snow and ice clinging to her hair, her long black dress fluttering in the wind like the dark, flapping wings of a crow.

Elijah had seen her many times, but unlike so many of the other ghosts that haunted the cemetery, she never once tried to speak to him.

Molly Fury was the loneliest ghost at Wellington.

When Noah told Lucy of his desperate plan to run away, she was apprehensive. Everyone at Wellington knew the stories. She thought of a compromise. Instead of Noah running away alone, they would all four run away for Christmas. It wouldn't really be running away; it would be more like a field trip. Lucy and Noah shared the simple plan with Elijah and Simon. They would sneak away on Christmas Eve night.

But where would they go? This time, Simon had the solution.

"What about that old barn in the field across the highway?" he asked, scratching his shorn head.

They all agreed.

The barn was perfect. It was not too far. They could sneak off to it and return first thing the following morning. Besides, there was something fitting about spending Christmas in a barn. They excitedly formulated their plans during dinner, in between bites of coagulating Salisbury steak, one of the most predictable food items on the dinner menu. They would gather supplies—blankets, matches and candles, food, and gifts—and sneak away after bed check the night before Christmas. They would spend the night in the barn and return Christmas morning.

All four loved the idea. Somehow, just having the plan made them happier, made the tedious days pass quickly. Before they knew it, the day of their temporary escape arrived.

In between breakfast and lunch on Christmas Eve, Noah and Elijah, seen by no one, noiselessly made their way into the laundry and swiped four dark-blue blankets. They knew that it would be cold in the barn and that the single blanket issued for each room would not be enough. At the same time, more or less, Lucy and Simon crept into the kitchen and took a package of frozen hot dogs and some raw biscuits that had already been rolled out and cut into circles. Lucy swiped a box of matches sitting on one of the large, industrial cooking stoves. At lunch and then again at dinner, each of the friends grabbed an extra apple or banana. They stashed everything in Simon's room until it was late enough to sneak away. That night, the boys played cards in Simon's room until it was bedtime, while Lucy lay reading on her bed.

Later that night, after the floor monitors were asleep, Noah, Simon, and Elijah escaped their dormitory, creeping down the flight of stairs without stepping on a single loose floorboard. By then, the boys knew which steps were tattle-tales and which ones could be trusted to keep a secret. No one noticed them crossing the dark lobby except a lone shrew darting across the hardwood floor, vanishing beneath a bookcase in the lobby, and a spider high up in a corner with one long leg resting on its web, waiting for vibrations. Elijah quietly pushed open the window, which he had unlocked during the day. One by one, all three boys tossed out their bundles of bedding and climbed through the opening.

Outside, the treacherous night was in a fit. A blizzard was forecast. Even though the snow had not yet begun, temperatures had dropped all through the day into the teens, and the wind was blowing so hard that large branches were breaking off trees. Already, a heavy branch had fallen onto the headmaster's new car, denting the roof and shattering the windshield. Dark black clouds hung so low from the sky that they seemed touchable. It hadn't snowed in over a week, but the ground was hardened by a white crust of old snow. On the walkways, a rind of salt marked thousands of footprints faintly visible crisscrossing the cobbled walkways of the school grounds.

The three friends gathered themselves behind the scraggly bushes beneath the dorm window. Noah looked above him and saw that the window was still open. He quickly stood up to close the window, which at first stuck in the frame and then banged shut. Just then, two security guards walked past the corner of the building, on the sidewalk. They stopped. The guards were close enough that the boys could hear their conversation despite the loud wind.

"Did you hear something?" the shorter man said as he flashed a light toward the dormitory.

The boys held their position behind the wind-quivering bushes, holding their breath, like rabbits making themselves invisible to sniffing dogs and coyotes.

"Just this damn wind," the taller of the two men said, pulling his cap low over his ears. "Whatya' get your kid for Christmas?"

"I got him a BB gun and a jack knife. What'd you get for yours?"

The second man had a higher voice.

"I got him one of them electric trains and a new baseball glove."

Twice more the searching light lit the brick walls near the boys' hiding place, but eventually the men and their light moved on into the darkness, the boys' safety restored as the light of the bobbing flashlight diminished. All three boys seemed to begin breathing again at the same time.

Simon was the first to speak.

"Let's go get Lucy."

Each picked up his bundle, swung it over a shoulder, and crept against the building, leaning into the stiff wind, ducking beneath each window they passed. At the end of the building, they huddled close, looking in every direction before running across the field toward Lucy's dormitory.

When she saw her friends crossing the white field, Lucy crawled out the same window she had used before, pulled it closed, and waited.

"You got everything?" Noah asked when he had come beside her.

Lucy nodded, picked up her own dark blue bundle, and turned her coat collar up. Her eyes were already watering from the stinging wind.

"Right here," she replied eagerly as she swung it over her tiny shoulder.

The quartet of young friends—best friends—worked their way across the campus, through the night, past the cemetery, and under the wrought-iron gates. They crossed the quiet road and pushed across the farmer's frozen field, their footprints mingling with the small, sharp tracks of deer.

At the far end of the field, the old barn leaned against the darkness, its fading red stain almost beautiful against the thin white snow and the dark clouds tangling themselves in tree branches at the edge of the forest.

The secret dancing place lay about a mile to the east.

When the four friends arrived at the barn, they stood before the dilapidated structure, stunned by its shaggy loneliness. They had never been this close to it, having seen it only from afar. The gabled roof still retained most of its split-shake shingles, but there were a few large holes from missing or rotted shakes. Only one of the small glass windows remained intact; all the rest had been broken. The front door hung loosely, held by a single long-strap hinge. Some of the red-stained planks cladding the outside of the barn were missing, allowing the wind to howl through the spaces like a pack of wolves. The old barn was a picture of decay and ruin.

But at least it wasn't Wellington.

Elijah pushed open the door, which broke from its remaining hinge and fell heavily to the floor. The inside of the barn didn't seem as bad as the outside. Only a little snow had filtered in, mostly from the few holes in the roof. There were still piles of old straw in the stables, brown and rotten on the exposed surface. Lucy scooped an armful of the exposed straw and tossed it aside. Underneath, the straw was still golden yellow and dry. There would be plenty for their beds. Noah and Simon looked around for firewood. They found old planks from the walls and flooring, boards from the stables, and old, buckled beams—uprights—which had supported the hay loft. Roof shingles made of cedar were scattered all about. In spite of the cold and darkness, the decay and ruin, the old barn smelled of cedar and straw and of better days gone by.

They prepared for the long, cold night by building great piles of clean straw for bedding, piling up firewood, and leaning the heavy door back into place to keep out the unwelcome wind. They even shored up several of the broken windows with pieces of old plywood, once used to patch a small area of plank flooring in what at one time had apparently been a tack room.

After a while a blazing fire, nestled inside a circle of old foundation stones, lit the inside of the barn, warming it. The four friends sat around the flames roasting hot dogs and telling jokes and scary stories. Later, as the fire dwindled, they talked for hours about home and about Christmases past, taking turns to feed the dying flames.

In the larger scheme of the threatening night, their little fire was a pathetic point of light, and despite their best attempts to seal their little world in the old barn, the cold crept in. But no matter how much the wind tried to wriggle through the cracks or around the tilted door to penetrate their refuge, the night was filled with warmth. For the first time in several months, Noah, Lucy, Elijah, and Simon were happy. They had escaped their captors. In this long-abandoned place they were free.

When it was bedtime, the boys each piled up straw along an interior wall of what had once been a stall. The wall against the outside was fairly solid—only a few small, rotted holes—and the wind didn't whistle since it was blowing against the other side of the barn. Lucy had discovered a wall box on the other side of the same interior wall, a V-shaped feeding trough attached to the wall by means of nails through the trough's topmost slat and from below by means of two angled support boards, one at each end, fixed from the outer edge of the trough to the base of the wall. One of the nails was exposed a little, and Lucy could see that its head was square, suggesting its ancient age.

She filled the trough with clean straw and depressed the mass along the center line of the trough, so that the straw looked not only like a mattress but like a blanket, inviting her into a warm cocoon. Though the feed trough was only a little over four feet long, it fit Lucy just right if she curled her knees slightly.

Curious at all the sound of fuss and arrangement coming from the other side of the wall, the three boys peered around the corner to find Lucy comfortably curled under her blanket in what looked, for all the world, like a high-dollar railroad-car berth. The three boys gathered around their friend, admiring her ingenuity.

"You comfortable, Lucy?" Elijah asked, feeling more and more like a proud older brother.

"Just right," Lucy replied, snuggling down even further into the pliant straw and beneath her dark-blue blanket.

The three boys winked and smiled at each other, found their own straw piles, and, having piled more wood onto the crackling fire, pulled their own blankets to their noses and waited for sleep to come.

They slept soundly, dreaming happy dreams filled with decorated trees, images of family, and brightly wrapped gifts.

In the early morning, while they slow-roasted biscuits at the ends of sticks held strategically above the fire, the friends exchanged gifts. Each had brought something to give, small pieces of pottery or drawings they had made in art class, something carved in wood shop, or something personal brought from home. The gifts had no monetary worth like a BB gun or an electric train or a jack knife, but they were priceless nonetheless.

When it was Lucy's turn to pass out gifts, she sat for a long time staring into the fire, holding her biscuit at the end of a stick above the flames. Finally, she spoke.

"My gift is a story my mother used to tell me. It's the story of how Raven brought light to the world."

As she began to speak, tears welled up in her eyes, slowly dripped down her cheeks.

The three boys looked away from her face, into the fire, not in shame but in compassion; they felt the hurt in their young friend. Lucy was the youngest of them, and although she had strength belying her age and small size, they knew how much she missed her mother.

Lucy told her story, slowly, the way elders tell such stories, holding to certain words, allowing time to absorb them, to discover the meaning.

"It was dark in the beginning. Everything was dark. People lived in the blackness, having never seen the world or one another. Raven had heard of a chief who, it was said, had three boxes of treasure. One box contained the stars, another held the moon, and the largest, most ornately carved box held the sun."

By now the boys were listening carefully, looking at Lucy. Noah placed another biscuit on the end of his stick and held it above the flames.

"Raven flew to the village and watched from a tree. When he saw the chief's daughter come down to the creek to drink water, Raven turned himself into a pine needle, which fell into the creek and floated downriver toward the girl, who dipped her wooden ladle into the fresh water. She did not notice the small, green pine needle floating on the surface when she took a long drink, swallowing Raven inside her."

By now Elijah, too, had placed another biscuit on his stick and held it at just the right height above the red and yellow flames. Simon studied his biscuit. It was almost ready.

"The chief's daughter became pregnant. A month later she gave birth to a baby boy, which was really Raven in disguise. She loved her son, and the chief loved his grandson. The baby quickly grew into a young boy, who cried and cried to play with the box containing the stars. Tired of his crying, the chief let his grandson have it, warning him not to open it. But as soon as Raven received the box he opened it, releasing the stars, which flew up through the smokehole and settled into the black sky."

Shadows cast by the fire flickered against the walls and the high roof of the old, dilapidated barn.

"The chief was angry that the boy had lost his treasure, but he loved his grandson; so when he cried to play with the box containing the moon, the old man gave in and gave him the carved cedar box. As quickly as he had released the stars, Raven opened the lid and freed the moon, which rose through the smokehole and took its place in the night sky. Now, for the first time, people could almost see the outlines of the world in which they lived."

Lucy paused to check her own biscuit. It was light brown, which meant that it was nearly ready.

"Having released the stars and the moon, Raven turned his eyes toward the largest box, the box of daylight. He cried and cried, but the chief would not give it to him. That night, when the whole village slept, Raven turned himself back into a black bird, crept up to the great box, and lifted the heavy lid. As the sun began to rise up through the smokehole, the chief awoke and tried to catch his treasure. But the sun flew into the sky, and the whole world was bright. For the first time, people could clearly see mountains and rivers and trees and each other. Raven flew away while the chief sat on his empty box, sad that he had lost his treasures, sadder still that he had lost his beloved grandson, who was nowhere to be found. Just then, a ray of sunlight fell through the smokehole, and the chief held his hand in the light, felt its warmth, and knew that it was good and that it was meant to be shared with the world."

Lucy smiled when she finished telling her gift, her small cheeks streaked with tears.

None of the boys spoke.

Outside, dark clouds lightened. The wind died altogether. Gently, without a sound, snowflakes began to fall. And some-how—miraculously—in the stillness of the new day, amid the quiet of the barn, the Spirit of the Season came and sat beside the fire.

Christmas had arrived after all.

Chapter Ten

THE FEMALE APPARITION standing at the far end of the otherwise empty gang showers in the boys' locker room was the second adult ghost Elijah had ever seen. She was wearing ragged clothes, a pair of yellowish leather moccasins with beaded floral patterns on the top, and her hair was long and black with strands of gray streaking through the dark mass. She didn't look too old. Maybe forty, Elijah thought, though he couldn't really tell. One thing was for sure: the woman was Indian. The odor of wood smoke filled the shower room. After looking around, the ghost floated into the locker area, full of boys changing into their clothes, some still standing around naked or in their underwear, one boy snapping a wet towel in the direction of a nearby friend.

Elijah followed the apparition, a towel wrapped around his waist. She hadn't noticed him, which was strange, he thought, since other ghosts always seemed so attracted to him. Instead, she drifted through the noisy room looking for something . . . or someone. She even stood on tiptoes to look over one closed door of a toilet stall. Elijah had seen Billy Tall Mountain heading into the stall a few moments earlier.

Elijah laughed aloud.

Good thing Billy couldn't see her.

After searching the room, the ghost with gray-streaked hair seemed to pour out a half-open window. Elijah watched as she crossed the broad, snow-covered lawn toward the administration building, passing through two teachers walking out the front door.

Elijah saw her again twice that week, wandering the halls of his dormitory one night and looking around the carpentry shop, even checking beneath the table saw and behind the wood planer.

"PLEASE TURN to page seventy-five," announced Miss Creger, the new history teacher, quickly turning the pages of her own book.

At just that moment, a loud siren began to wind up until it reached a constant shriek, announcing a Civil Defense drill, a precaution in the event of nuclear attack.

"Everyone! Everyone!" the teacher shouted, clapping, trying to be heard over the piercing wail. "Please assume the proper position under your desks."

All the students in the classroom scooted out from their chairs and crawled under their desks, tucking in legs and arms until each was huddled, turtle-like, lest any part be exposed to a nuclear blast or radiation. Lucy hated the drills. She knew, even at fourteen, that such a posture was futile. She had seen black-and-white photographs of Hiroshima and Nagasaki in a book she found in the library. The rubble in those photographs included no desks, no chairs, no buildings—only rubble, only the suggestion, the outlines, of where buildings once stood.

This was a stupid exercise, she thought.

The students waited beneath the false safety of their desktops until the siren ceased and the headmaster announced the all-clear on the intercom. A few minutes later, the classroom having returned to normal, a student office helper poked his head in the door and handed Miss Creger a note.

The two exchanged whispers.

Miss Creger seemed shaken. She was young and beautiful and

thin. Wellington was her first teaching position. She seemed to enjoy her job, to enjoy teaching children. That the students at Wellington were Indian didn't seem to matter to her. She even shared with her students something of her personal life—how she spent her summers, jokes her sister shared with her in her letters. She told them how she came to be at Wellington. For her, it wasn't a last-option choice; it's where she wanted to teach. She had applied during her last semester at a teacher's college in northeast Missouri. She was elated when she received her letter of appointment from the headmaster. During the weekends, Miss Creger usually drove into town to spend time with friends she had made in the area and to dance at the local gathering places. She loved to dance. The students liked her fine. She was a good teacher and, to the students, a real person, someone from whom they could learn and to whom they could openly respond, which was a rare thing at the school.

When the office helper left, Miss Creger turned toward the class, looking for a face. "Lucy," she said with a smile. "Can you come up front, please?"

Lucy wondered why she was being called to the front of the class. She wondered what the note said. She hadn't done anything wrong. She was sure of it, at least mostly sure.

Miss Creger took Lucy aside and spoke in a low voice, trying to maintain her cheerfulness, though Lucy could see that the woman was forcing her smile, that she hid something behind the upturned corners of her pretty lips.

"Lucy, you need to go speak to the counselor. Take this note with you," she said, patting Lucy on the shoulder as she led her out the door, closing it softly as Lucy walked down the center of the long, empty hall.

As she walked along, slowly, hearing her footsteps echoing against the polished-cement floor and block walls, Lucy studied the note. Nothing in its handwritten contents explained why she was being called. It simply stated that "Lucy Secondchief is to report to the counselor immediately." When she arrived, Lucy stood outside the dark wood-and-glass door for several moments, holding the note in both hands, reading it again and again, as if she had missed something.

Finally, she knocked lightly.

"Come in," said a man's voice from inside.

Lucy opened the door and stood in the entrance. A man in a brown suit with a brown-and-yellow-striped tie was sitting in the corner of a beige-colored cloth sofa, holding a piece of pale-yellow paper in one hand. The paper was thin and showed the effects of several folds. It looked almost transparent, and Lucy could make out lines of typed script.

"Are you Lucy Secondchief?"

"Yessir."

"Come in, Lucy. Sit down," he continued, leaning to his left and patting the surface of the sofa with his left hand.

Lucy walked over to the sofa, looking around the small office and at the framed diplomas and certificates hanging on the walls. Against one wall were several shelves full of books. They all seemed neatly ordered, fitted precisely into their spaces. She had never been in this office before, nor had she ever seen the man around school.

Lucy sat down, nervously, still holding the handwritten note.

The man picked up a mug of hot coffee from a little table just to the right of the sofa, sipping twice before replacing the cup in the center of its coaster. He cleared his throat before speaking.

"I'm afraid I have some bad news, Lucy. Your mother is dead. She died last week. I'm sorry to have to be the one to tell you this. The telegram arrived only today. These things take time."

He held up the piece of paper.

"Is there anyone you'd like to call?" he asked, reaching for a pad and pencil.

At first, Lucy did not understand the words. After several moments she realized she was not breathing. Then she breathed. Then she understood. There was no one else. Lucy had no parents now, no family at all. She was alone.

"No sir," she finally replied.

After a brief pause, the man said, "You may go to your dorm room, if you'd like. You're exempt from classes for the rest of the day." Then, looking at his wristwatch, he added, "I have another student coming in any minute, so if that's all," he said, standing up and extending his right hand to pat Lucy on the shoulder. "I wish you luck. Everything will be okay."

Lucy left the office. She didn't want to sit in her dorm room alone, so she went back to class. On entering, she didn't look at Miss Creger. She didn't look at anyone, though everyone was looking at her. Instead, she spent the rest of the hour staring out the window, not hearing a single thing, not even the bell announcing lunch time. After the other students had left for the cafeteria, Miss Creger sat down at the desk next to Lucy, who was still staring out the window.

"I'm sorry about your mother," she said softly.

Lucy didn't respond at first, but the teacher could see the little girl's eyes well with tears. Finally, she reached for Miss Creger's hand. For several minutes the two sat looking out the window.

Miss Creger broke the silence.

"Tell me about your mother."

Throughout the entire lunch hour, Lucy held hands with her teacher and told the story of her life with her mother. She talked about how she had lost her father, how she and her mother had struggled. She talked about their bedtime routine and about rabbits and the day the men came and took her away. Through tears, and almost unable to speak, Lucy described the last time she saw her mother—running behind the black car, slipping and falling in the mud. At times as she told the story, Lucy laughed and smiled. But mostly, she sobbed, her whole body trembling.

LUCY WAS QUIET and withdrawn for the rest of the week. Even after. Not even her friends could bring her out of her melancholy, though they tried. Lucy hardly ate. She went to bed early, crying herself to sleep. Sometimes, she stood in the shower for long stretches, momentarily comforted by the reassuring embrace of hot water.

Ever since her arrival, Lucy had seen Wellington as the place, the thing, that had taken her away from her mother, and now it seemed that it had taken her mother away from her. She was empty inside, and none of her friends could help.

Some wells are bottomless.

One Saturday, after she had finally stopped crying, Lucy reluctantly joined her friends ice skating on the pond at the lowest portion of the school grounds, beyond the old maintenance building where Simon had endured his punishment. She had borrowed a pair of skates—a size too big—from a girl who was sick with a cold. Slowly, with a kind of methodical certainty, she laced on the skates and glided, after a fashion, to the edge of the icy activity.

A stream along the woods at the edge of the school property emptied into the pond at the near end, swelling its sides and filling its depth. At the far end, the stream poured over a kind of spillway, and then resumed its course through the county for another sixteen miles, passing through farms and two small towns. Both pond and stream were frozen over, providing a sizable area for skating.

Several children were out on the pond, including a few girls in regular shoes, but mostly boys in hockey skates. Only a few students owned skates, but they took turns. Several boys were playing hockey with makeshift equipment: two-by-fours for sticks and a rock for a puck; and a few girls twirled and twirled in white-shoed figure skates. Most of the children just stood around talking, while others were running and sliding across the ice in their street shoes.

The pond was quite deep from the middle toward the earthen dam that held back the water to a depth of seven or eight feet. At the far end of the dam, near where the stream left the pond over the spillway, signs warned, "Danger! Thin Ice."

Noah, Elijah, and Simon were busy racing one another on borrowed skates, when Lucy wobbled unsteadily away. No one noticed her skating slowly and deliberately toward the signs.

After easily winning the sprint, Simon looked around for Lucy, who usually applauded the winner. She wasn't standing where they had left her. He looked across the pond, searching for her amid the many boys and girls skating or playing or standing around talking and laughing. Noah was the first to see her.

"Over there!" he yelled, pointing to the far side of the pond, toward the warning signs, where he could see a dark hole in the ice, thin ice fragments, glass-like, floating on the surface, still swelling from some recent motion in the water, just where he no longer saw Lucy.

All three boys sped to the hole. Noah and Simon stopped where the ice became too thin to support their weight, but Elijah kept going, the surface splintering spider-web-like beneath him. Other students, turning in the direction of the commotion, skated or ran or slid toward them, curious and afraid.

Elijah dropped onto his belly and pulled himself to the very edge of the dark opening, his arms and legs spread, distributing his weight as evenly as possible so that, he hoped, he wouldn't break through.

Noah turned to the nearby students. "Give me your coats!" he shouted, pulling off his own. Several boys handed him their winter jackets. Noah started tying them together by their sleeves. Seeing what his friend was doing, Simon helped. They quickly tied a ten-foot lifeline made of multicolored coats.

More students approached, standing on the safe side of the signs. Some were asking who fell in, others wondered how Lucy could have missed the signs, and several girls stood with their hands pressed against their face, anxious, beginning to cry.

Elijah reached into the icy water with one arm, shoulder deep, feeling around for Lucy.

"Lucy! Lucy!" His frantic voice called over and over.

Noah and Simon tried to inch closer to the hole, but every time they did, they could hear the sharp snapping of ice, could see fracture lines race across the surface. They stepped back.

Finally, his arm and hand freezing, Elijah felt something and pulled it up. A mat of long, black, gray-streaked hair floated to the surface. He reached into the mass of hair with both hands to lift her out when the head rolled up from beneath the dark water. Instead of Lucy's face, it was the ghostly face of the Indian woman he had seen around the school. Her eyes were wide open, pupiless, gray-white and lifeless. Terrified, Elijah recoiled, releasing his hold. The head and hair sank, returning into the darkness. Elijah was terrified, afraid to reach again into the black water, certain that the ghost wanted to drag him beneath the ice.

Just then, a head again floated to the surface, its long, black hair floating like seaweed. Elijah cautiously reached for the head, ready to pull back in an instant. He grabbed a handful of black hair and slowly pulled. This time Lucy's face emerged to greet him, her eyes closed, her skin chalky white. Elijah was sure she was dead, that the ghost had lured her to the thin ice and drowned her. He tried to pull her from the water. But the ice broke from the added weight, and Elijah plunged into the freezing pond with Lucy, splashing with his one free hand, trying to stay afloat while holding on to his friend at the same time. The water was so cold that he almost couldn't breath.

Noah tossed Elijah one end of the rope of coats and yelled, "Grab hold!"

Simon cupped his hands around his mouth and shouted, "Grab the rope!"

Noah tossed it three times before Elijah could reach it. Then, as he held on to Lucy, Simon and Noah pulled. Inch by inch, they dragged Elijah and Lucy out of the water and across the surface until they were safely onto thick ice.

Several more boys took off their coats and wrapped them around Lucy's still, unbreathing body and around Elijah, who was shivering uncontrollably, his teeth clicking in a ghostly, wordless chatter. By then, Miss Creger had arrived on the frantic scene. She knelt beside Lucy, listening for a heartbeat and for signs of breathing. Everyone was quiet. All the girls were crying. Elijah stood nearby, shaking beneath a drape of several coats, water dripping from his clothes. The fretful teacher looked up at the students surrounding her.

They knew from her worried expression that Lucy wasn't breathing.

But Miss Creger was unwilling to give up. She told Noah to bend Lucy's legs to her stomach while she pinched her nose closed between two fingers and breathed into her mouth. While Noah pumped the lifeless legs up and down, Miss Creger filled Lucy's lungs with her own warm breath, until Lucy coughed and spat out a lung full of pond water. She coughed several more times. Then she opened her eyes and lay quiet, staring at gray clouds floating across a distant blue-gray sky, smiling, oblivious to the many relieved faces looking down at her. At Miss Creger's instruction, Simon and Noah helped Lucy to her unsteady feet, and, with their arms around her for support, delivered her to the Nurse's office.

The next day, Lucy was allowed to have visitors. Her body temperature had returned to normal, and she was feeling stronger. Around her bed, piled high with blankets, stood her three rescuers. A cup of chicken broth sat on a nearby table. The school nurse had told Lucy how her friends had saved her, how Elijah almost drowned in the attempt.

Lucy thanked them for what they had done, receiving a gentle hug from each.

"Boy, we thought you were a goner for sure," Simon said, holding Lucy's hand.

"Don't ever scare us like that again," Noah said, patting her on the head, the way he often did.

Elijah said nothing when it was his turn to hug her, but his embrace was tighter and lasted longer than the others.

The four talked for a while, telling jokes and laughing, until the nurse told them it was time to go. As the three boys turned to leave, Lucy asked them to stay for a moment.

"It was a strange thing," she said, looking away from her friends and out the window at steel-gray clouds. "After I blacked out, I saw my mother. She was in the water with me. She swam up from below and grabbed my arm and pushed me to the surface. She saved me. The nurse said I must have been dreaming or imagining, but it wasn't a dream. It wasn't."

Elijah hadn't told anyone about the woman in the pond or the apparition in the showers. And no one asked why Lucy had skated past the signs and onto thin ice, beyond the warning signs, to where the ice turned to a black hole of danger and darkness.

Chapter Eleven

"LISTEN, I'VE SEEN HIM RUN, and I'm telling you, Simon can run faster than all of them." Elijah spoke proudly to Noah, on his left, and to Lucy, on his right, as the three friends sat on the bottom row of the bleachers overlooking the track field full of boys stretching or jogging back and forth along the near straightaway of the quarter-mile track. Simon stood before them, awkwardly, at the edge of the track, feeling the warming spring sunshine on his skin. He was blowing a plucked dandelion, watching the seeds disperse and gently float away.

"No one can run like Simon," Elijah concluded with a kind of finality.

"Is that true, Simon? Are you faster than all these guys?" Noah asked.

Simon stood by, fumbling for a proper posture just in front and to the left of his friends, on the edge of the cinder-path track that encircled the football field. He had been watching the older boys warming up. One of his shoes was untied, and his turned-up jeans cuffs exposed his brown socks. Simon looked down at his feet while replying.

"I don't know 'bout that," he replied, shyly.

"Hell, Simon. I know you can beat 'em," Elijah boasted. "You can run faster than a horse!"

Mr. Moody, the track coach, was standing a few feet away, his shiny whistle hanging on a string around his neck. He was one of the oldest teachers at Wellington, overweight by fifty or sixty pounds, with a thick, gray mustache that half covered the hole of his mouth like a gabled roof of thatch. From where he stood he could hear the conversation.

Lucy leaned forward to see Simon better. He was still looking down at his feet, a little smile on his lips. "Simon? Are you really that fast?"

"C'mon, Simon, are you?" Noah prodded.

By now the track coach had moved closer to the four friends, his interest piqued.

Simon replied without looking up. "Yeah, I guess it's true," he said.

"What's your name, son?" Coach Moody asked, facing Simon, both hands on his hips.

"Lone Fight," Simon whispered, thinking he was in some kind of trouble. Usually, when a teacher asked for a student's name, it was for punishment.

"I hear you're a runner. How come I didn't see you at tryouts?" Simon was visibly uncomfortable.

"I just like to run, that's all. I never ran on no team."

"How about showing me what you got, kid?" Mr. Moody asked, though it sounded more like a command. He turned around and blasted his whistle toward the field.

"Varsity Team!" he shouted. "Line up!"

Seven older boys, all taller and more developed than Simon, gathered in front of the coach.

"This here is Lone Fight," he said, motioning to Simon. "I wanna see what he's got. Let's see . . . I want you three to race him." He pointed to his three fastest runners. One of them had participated in the previous spring's state four-forty championship.

Moody led Simon over to the starting line. Noah, Elijah, and

Lucy climbed off of the bleachers and stood along the track to watch. All the other boys and half a dozen spectators gathered to watch as the three varsity runners took their starting positions.

With one hand on Simon's shoulder, the fat coach guided the young Indian to his position, in lane four, the outside of the four lanes to be used, each lane marked with old pieces of white-painted wood lined end-to-end around the track and embedded deeply on edge among the cinders.

"One lap around this here track is 440 yards. You stay in this lane," he said, pointing to the vague white-painted lines separating the lanes, visible beneath the light coating of cinders. "When I blow this whistle, you run as fast as you can around the track, but stay inside your lane."

Simon had never seen a formal track race before, on an oval track with painted lines. He didn't know that runners were normally staggered for races longer than one hundred yards, instead of lined up side by side.

The other boys crouched in a near-sprinting position, one arm extended, one arm back. Simon just stood there, upright, in his long pants, as the coach stepped off the track. Simon's shoe was still untied. He hadn't even stretched or warmed up. Then again, Simon didn't know how to stretch or warm up. He just knew how to run.

Mr. Moody raised the whistle close to his lips. In the other hand he held up a stopwatch, his thumb perched at the ready.

"Ready, set . . ." And then he blew the shrill whistle, simultaneously pressing the small button on the stopwatch.

Simon was so startled by the whistle's piercing screech that he jumped a little and turned to look at Coach Moody. The three track-team members threw themselves down the track, their heads bent down, their teeth clinched, fierce looks of determination in their eyes. They were a dozen steps down the track before Simon understood what was happening.

"Run, Simon!" Lucy and Elijah yelled, motioning toward the other runners.

Confused, Simon finally bolted like a surprised jackrabbit. Just before entering the first turn, his left shoe flew off his foot. He stopped to pick it up, losing time, then carried it the rest of the way like a smelly baton. He ran the course of the oval track wearing only one shoe, smiling the whole time, never once changing the easy pace of his breathing. He loved the way his muscles felt pushing him against the wind, the way his heart beat out a drum song, the way his mind cleared the longer he ran.

Midway down the backstretch, Simon pulled up alongside the third of the three boys. He slowed his pace slightly and looked into the taller boy's face. He liked what he saw, an agony of effort, a desperate breathing.

By the time the state championship competitor, a few yards ahead of the second boy, was in the apex of the far turn, between the goal posts of the football field, Simon was dead even with him, matching him stride for stride, the older boy in the inside-most lane, Simon out in lane four. When they came out of the turn and into the final stretch, Simon was five yards ahead of the older boy, despite his late start, still smiling, still breathing evenly, even when he flashed by Moody, fifteen yards ahead of his fastest runner.

The coach ran out to embrace Simon.

"My God, Son! I've never seen anything like that. You just possibly broke the state record!" he exclaimed, holding the stopwatch close to Simon's face.

Lucy, Noah, and Elijah surrounded Simon, patting him on the back and congratulating him.

"I told you he was fast," Elijah blurted proudly.

A group of students practicing baseball at an adjacent field came over to see what was going on, intrigued by all the commotion.

"That was something!" someone yelled.

"Who was that?" someone asked.

The last of the three runners finally crossed the finish line, each, in turn, catching his breath, holding a hand against his side, walking off the burning in his thighs.

Mr. Moody grabbed Simon by the shoulders, shaking him enthusiastically.

"Amazing! Do you think you could do that again?" he asked, worried that the race might have been a fluke. Perhaps his stopwatch was broken. Perhaps the other three runners purposefully ran slowly to let Simon win by such a margin. Perhaps he was dreaming.

Simon liked the attention. No one back home thought much of his running.

"I think I could go a little faster this time . . . my shoe coming off and all."

By now, another couple dozen students had gathered around the field. A few boys were running around telling everyone about the race. Pretty soon, almost a hundred students, teachers, and a groundskeeper were standing around waiting to see Simon run. Even Headmaster Dichter, who had been walking between buildings, came to watch. He was surprised and a little chagrined when he learned it was Simon, that insolent boy who refused to break under his punishment. Moody led the headmaster away from the growing crowd, and although Noah, Lucy, and Elijah couldn't hear what they were talking about, they knew from the way they kept looking at Simon that they were planning how best to make use of the new star.

When their conference was over, Mr. Moody picked three fresh boys to race against Simon. The original three were still catching their breath. Simon double-tied the strings of his brown street shoes and crouched like the other runners, imitating their starting position. This time, when the whistle signaled, he exploded down the track without a wasted second.

Almost two hundred people chanted his name from along the edge of the track.

"SI-MON! SI-MON! SI-MON!" They chanted faster and faster as he picked up speed, pouring it on like a dragster until it runs out of track.

When Simon crossed the finish line, the boys behind him hadn't even reached the backstretch. Seeing him so far ahead, they just quit running. It wasn't even a race. Might as well as pit a man against a thoroughbred.

The overweight, sweat-shirted coach lumbered onto the track again.

"Unbelievable!" he shouted, holding out a hand. "I need you on my team. Just think of what you could do for our school! We could go all the way. You could take us to state . . . the nationals. Hell," he half-whispered with tears forming at the corner of both eyes, "the Olympics."

The coach, as best he could, was jumping for joy. "Yessiree! You could take me all the way to the Olympics," he said, enthusiastically pumping Simon's hand while thinking about Jim Thorpe and a glass case full of trophies.

Even Headmaster Dichter, his comb-over all awry, congratulated Simon.

"By God, Son, you'll make our school proud."

Simon looked away from the field. He saw the school buildings, the dorms, the maintenance shed where he had been held prisoner. From where he stood, he could even see the wrought-iron gates at the entrance, the sign welcoming him and his friends, welcoming the older boys he had just humiliated—whose humiliation had now turned to admiration—to Wellington.

He turned to the coach and pulled his hand free.

"No thank you, Sir," he said, so quietly that most of the crowd around them could not hear.

Then he walked away, his friends joining him, walking alongside, talking about how fast he was.

The bewildered coach stood at the edge of the track watching his future cross the green toward the cafeteria. Unable to fathom the meaning, he stood for a long time staring at the hands of the stopwatch, frozen in time the way the moment would be forever frozen in his mind.

Chapter Twelve

THE YELLOW SCHOOL BUS was nearly full when Noah Boyscout stepped aboard, and the tall, skinny driver pulled the squeaking lever, closing the folding metal-and-glass door. He smiled and nodded at Miss Creger, who was sitting on the first seat. She was coming along as a chaperone. As the bus lurched forward, Noah walked down the narrow aisle, swaying from side to side, grabbing the seat-backs on both sides to steady himself.

Midway, he saw Arthur Pretty Shield sitting alone by a window. Arthur was in Noah's carpentry class, one of the classes required for older boys learning how to build things with two-by-fours and plywood. The school had long ago decided that Indian boys needed to know how to build things, so that when they returned to their reservations they could build modern houses with shingled roofs and white picket fences and small square decks for barbecue grills and lawn chairs, houses like all the new houses sprouting up like dandelions in the American suburbs.

Indian boys didn't need algebra or trigonometry. They needed geometry, the mathematics of angles and squareness and roof pitches. That's how young Indian men were to join the mainstream, with a hammer in one hand and a measuring tape in the other. Indian girls focused primarily on domestic classes—sewing, cooking, etiquette. They learned how to use electric vacuum cleaners, dishwashers, laundry machines, and ovens; they learned which fork went on which side of the table setting—useful knowledge for housewives . . . or maids.

Noah looked toward the back of the bus and saw that all the seats were taken. He didn't want to sit with Arthur. No one did. There was nothing physically wrong with Arthur. He didn't smell or anything. His offense was depression, which was persistent. Clinical. Contagious.

Arthur Pretty Shield was the most homesick Indian at Wellington.

Almost every time Noah had seen Arthur around school—in class, in the dorm, or in the cafeteria, the boy was hunched over a table, staring blankly or crying. More than crying—sobbing. Sometimes he was forced to wear a girl's dress all day long, one of the many demeaning and humiliating punishments for unruly boys. Reluctantly, Noah sat down beside Arthur, who seemed surprised and delighted that someone would sit with him.

"Want half?" Arthur asked, smiling meekly, pulling a tuna-fish sandwich from a brown paper bag.

Noah could smell it. He looked at it and at the trees and fields and houses flashing past the window. He felt nauseous.

"No thanks," he said, as kindly as he could.

Arthur ate his lunch. The smell made Noah sick. When Arthur was done eating, he nervously folded and unfolded the crinkling paper bag.

The inside of the bus was noisy with conversations. Miss Creger was leading some students in one of those never-ending songs. It was twenty miles to town, a half hour drive, more or less. The song would go on for a long time.

Midway, Arthur stopped fidgeting with his empty paper bag and leaned close to Noah.

"Why doesn't anyone like me?" he asked, his voice low and serious, his eyes hopeful. "I mean, how come no one ever sits with me or talks to me?"

Noah answered without looking at the other boy.

"I don't know," he replied, his voice defensive, his shoulders slightly shrugging.

He didn't want to talk, not about this.

Arthur realized he was treading dark water. He backed off a bit, allowing some distance between them.

"I guess what I'm asking," he continued, looking straight ahead, wringing his hands, "is, why is it people won't even talk to me?"

There was genuineness in his words . . . a lonely seriousness, like a wintered field, sad and barren—waiting for the sun.

Noah didn't respond for almost a mile. Instead, he looked out the window at the houses, which passed by more frequently now that the bus was close to town.

Finally, he turned toward Arthur, who was still wringing his hands.

"It's like this," Noah said, sensing the boy's desperation. "You're a drag. Nothing personal. But you're always crying. No one wants to be around that."

"But isn't everyone here sad? I mean, doesn't everyone want to go home?"

"Sure they do," Noah replied. "But crying doesn't change anything. You gotta show them that you're strong."

Arthur knew who "them" was.

"But I can't take it here. I miss my family. I miss my parents." His voice was beginning to break. He was about to cry. "Don't you miss your family?"

"Of course I do!" Noah's voice was growing angry. "Don't you think every kid on this bus would rather be home? Don't you think they're all homesick?"

Arthur kept his head down.

"I guess. But I can't take it anymore," he whispered, just loud enough to be heard.

Noah didn't respond.

"When do we go home?" asked Arthur, a great, billowing anxiety behind his question.

Noah thought carefully before he replied. He knew that a place like Wellington could destroy a spirit, rip it to shreds the way a grizzly bear rips apart a salmon. He remembered how he prayed that would not happen to Simon when he was chained to the storeroom wall.

"Look, none of us can change the way things are," he said as gently as he could. "Our parents can't change things. It's the law. So we have to be strong. We have to fight back. Resist. We have to make it through. You crying all the time reminds us where we are. Can't you see that?"

Arthur stopped rubbing his hands together, and although Noah couldn't see his face, he saw tears falling onto Arthur's lap, soaking into the neatly folded brown-paper bag.

Noah felt sorry for the boy. He wanted to say something useful.

"It ain't fair, that's for sure. I don't understand it myself. But there it is. It's just the way things are."

Neither spoke again for the rest of the ride. Arthur kept his head down, occasionally trembling and wiping tears from his face. Noah stared out the window, his jaw clenched, looking at the fields and the far hills, wishing he could be out there, alone, in the greening forests.

WHEN THE BUS PULLED INTO TOWN, the streets and sidewalks were busy with Saturday afternoon shoppers walking in and out of storefronts and diners, the corner grocery, the Five & Dime. A double feature was showing at the theater, their titles displayed on the marquee—both westerns.

Cowboys and Indians.

Indians always lost.

Wellington students were allowed to go into town once a

month to spend the meager allowances sent by their families. School officials kept careful records of who went each time. Many were prohibited from going, as another form of disciplinary punishment. Indeed, Simon had been caught speaking Navajo again, so he wasn't allowed to go. Instead, he was scrubbing bathroom floors with a toothbrush. Lucy was helping with preparations for the school dance, and Elijah, who wasn't feeling well, spent the day catching up on his sleep. Besides, like most of the other students, Elijah didn't have any money to spend in town anyhow. Those who did have some jingle in their pockets and were allowed to make the trip might spend their money on a movie or a burger and a soda. Some bought ice cream cones or malts or milkshakes. Some kids pooled their money and bought large pizzas, sitting together at a table adorned with a red-and-white-checkered tablecloth and a frothy pitcher of root beer.

Noah wanted to see a movie. He hadn't seen one in a long time. His parents had sent him a dollar, more than enough for the ticket and a small box of popcorn.

As the students rushed to get off the bus when the door swung open, filing out into the sunshine, Miss Creger shouted, "Remember to be back here no later than three o'clock! Three o'clock!"

It was almost noon. Noah walked quickly toward the theater. The feature started in ten minutes. Luckily, Arthur didn't follow him.

The movie, *North of the Great Divide* starring Roy Rogers, was less than two hours long, even with the news reel and two cartoons. When it was over, Noah joined three other school mates who had seen the same movie. Since the bus wouldn't leave for almost an hour, they talked about the film as they walked to the pizza parlor. One of the boys was doing a pretty good imitation of Iron Eyes Cody as they entered through the glass door, laughing. The four young Indians took one of the few remaining empty tables, still smiling and talking about the movie and deciding what they were going to order.

Noah was the first to notice that everyone in the whole place was staring at them, that he and his friends were the only Indians in the restaurant. Not a single person was talking. All eyes were on their table, all mouths frowning. It was so quiet that Noah thought he could actually hear his pride fall into the pit of his knotting stomach, like the silvery sound of a pebble dropped into calm water.

The other three Indians stopped what they were doing and looked around the hushed, angry room. Joshua Gray Hawk, a year older than Noah, the boy who a few moments before was comically imitating Iron Eyes Cody, straightened as tall as he could in his chair.

"What are you looking at?" he snarled at a family sitting at a nearby table, his gesture challenging the room, as though he had spent his entire life challenging the world—which, of course, he had.

Almost immediately the room returned to normal, filled with the sound of low conversations and silverware against plates. The waitress went back to taking orders and pouring water from a pitcher, while several men in a window booth kept turning around, scowling at the Indians and then returning to their conversation, occasionally looking back or pointing.

For ten minutes Noah and his schoolmates waited for the waitress to take their order. Then twenty. Each time she passed their table with a round tray of pizza or several sodas, they tried to catch her attention. She even took orders from two couples who came in well after the boys did. After half an hour, it became clear she had no intention of serving them at all.

Before leaving, Noah went to the bathroom. The walls were scribbled with the usual graffiti found in any men's room: "Call Debbie for a good time," "Kilroy was here," "Freddy loves Mabel," and brief limericks rhyming with various acts related to defecation. But above the urinal was scrawled something Noah hadn't expected to find. In big, black letters were four biting words: "Better dead than Red." Noah looked around. Beside the mirror someone had written, "The only good Injin is a dead Injin." And on the walls inside the toilet stall, was the warning, "Go Home Redskins!"

Noah wet a paper towel to erase the cutting words, but they persisted no matter how furiously he wiped and scrubbed. He snatched more towels and added soap to the mass of soggy, brown paper. But the words were indelible, stronger than any solvent, utterly resistant to friction, as if they were an actual part of the masonry or tile or steel on which they were scrawled. He gave up, angry and worn out. He hadn't asked to come here. None of the children at the school had asked for any of this.

Noah was visibly upset when he walked out of the men's room, quickly crossing the floor to his friends, still waiting at the table.

"Let's get outta here," he said, impatiently, motioning toward the door.

By the time the four boarded the bus, it was almost time to return to Wellington. They sat together in the back row. A few minutes later, Arthur Pretty Shield climbed the steps, found an empty seat in the middle, and sat down by himself.

"What got you so riled up?" Gray Hawk asked Noah, as the bus driver started the bus.

"Nothin'," replied Noah, looking out the window at all the townspeople coming and going, smiling warmly, nodding toward one other, and shaking hands on the street.

Miss Creger walked down the aisle, using a finger to take a head count.

"Everyone's here," she said to the driver, who closed the door and drove around the town square and back onto Main Street.

At the edge of town, the bus started sputtering. The engine was dying. The driver quickly turned into the parking lot of an old church, which had been built about the same time as Wellington.

The building's exterior was made of white-painted clapboards. The parking lot was half-filled with cars and pickup trucks. A large sign at the driveway entrance read, "Revival Today! Come Feel God's Love! Visitor's Welcome!"

Just as the bus cleared the church driveway, the engine sighed, coughed, and finally died with a shudder, like some child with tuberculosis. The driver turned the key half a dozen times, but the engine only clicked or made no sound at all. At least the bus was off the road. The driver told the kids to stay seated while he went outside. He lifted the heavy yellow hood and inspected the dead engine. He was a driver, not a mechanic. He didn't know the first thing about engines. He stood looking for something obvious, a disconnected spark plug wire or battery cable. He tried to jiggle the battery cables. Nothing appeared out of place. He even kicked a tire for good measure.

The inside of the bus was getting hot, even with the windows open, so Miss Creger directed the students to sit outside under some trees on the edge of the property while she went inside the church to call the school for help.

The sound of singing drifted across the parking lot from the open windows and front doors of the church.

Miss Creger walked through the open doors and addressed an elderly lady in a pink dress and a fine, wide-brimmed flowered hat.

"Afternoon, Ma'am," she said smiling. "Our bus broke down in your parking lot. I wonder if it would be an inconvenience if I used your telephone to call for help."

The woman looked over Miss Creger's shoulder, saw the broken down school bus with the word "Wellington" painted on the side. Several dozen Indian children were sitting on the lawn or standing and talking outside the bus.

Just then, a deacon stepped out from the double doors separating the sanctuary from the lobby. He had a hymnbook and a flyer in his hands. When he saw the pretty teacher he greeted her warmly.

"Glad to have you here, Sister," he said, shaking her hand and proffering the hymnbook. "Come join us."

The congregation began singing "Just a Closer Walk with Thee."

"No, no, Brother Jones," the lady in the yellow dress interrupted. "This woman is with another group," she said, nodding in the direction of the broken down bus.

The deacon glanced out the open door behind the driver and then back toward the woman.

"Her bus broke down. She needs a phone to call Wellington. I was just about to tell her . . ."

The deacon set the hymnbook on a nearby table.

"Sorry, but we don't have a phone here," he said. "Nearest one's at that service station about half mile back, where Elm Street crosses the highway.

The elderly woman confirmed quickly. "Yes, Elm Street. You know that Gulf Station, don't you? Ernie Turner's place."

"Yes, thank you for that, Ma'am," replied Miss Creger. "Do you think we could get some water? It's pretty hot today."

"Our faucet's broken," replied the deacon, looking down at his polished black shoes.

As Miss Creger walked out the door, she heard a phone ringing in the church office.

Outside, she told the bus driver, who volunteered to walk to the gas station.

"Now, you kids stay put," he said, before he started down the road. "Mind your teacher, and don't get in no trouble."

The driver hadn't been gone five minutes when three men, each dressed in their Sunday best, emerged from the church and crossed the parking lot to the bus, the benevolent words to "Amazing Grace" spilling out of the open church windows behind them.

"You fellas come give us a hand," Deacon Jones said, addressing group of older boys, including Noah, standing nearby. "We're gonna push this thing over there." He was pointing to a place on the other side of the highway.

One of the other men climbed inside the bus, sat down, released the parking brake, and shifted the gears into neutral.

"Go ahead!" he yelled out the side window.

The men and all the Indian boys, even a couple older girls, pushed the bus out the church entrance and across the road, where it came to rest on the narrow gravel shoulder, part of it still dangerously exposed on the asphalt, the bus pointing in the wrong direction.

Deacon Jones and the other men stuffed their starched shirt-tails back into their pants and adjusted their neck ties.

"That outta do it," he said, wiping dust from his hands. "Now you kids stay out of our parking lot. And mind the traffic."

Just then a semitruck passed, the driver blasting his horn.

"What's wrong with you people?" Miss Creger shouted as the deacon and the two other men crossed the highway. "This is a church, for chrissake!"

None of the three men looked back.

The kids sat around in the ditch alongside the road waiting for help to arrive. Some of the girls were picking dandelions. Noah sat down beneath a tree, leaned against its smooth trunk. The shade felt good. From where he sat, he could see the church sign. *Come Feel God's Love.*

Noah closed his eyes and fell asleep to the muffled sound of singing. In his dream, he was standing at the edge of a wide river. A grizzly bear sow and two cubs searched for salmon on the far shore, occasionally smacking the water with a fast paw. A young eagle soared overhead. Noah knew the place, knew where he was. He could see forested hills and white-capped mountains piling up in the distance. He was near his village, alone in the vast, wilderness, except that he wandered beneath trees that never grew in his village. In the pleasant dream, he walked along the river for almost a mile, alternately resting in a meadow of yellow flowers and tromping through drifts of powdery snow, until he slumped forward, waking himself.

Groggy, Noah looked around, his eyes adjusting to the brightness. The tranquil dream was lost. The bears and eagle vanished. The hills and mountains flattened into the rolling highway, and the meadow of yellow flowers resolved into the school bus.

For the first time in months, Noah began to cry. He wiped his eyes quickly before anyone noticed. When he looked up again, he saw Arthur Pretty Shield sitting with his back against a rear tire of the bus, his head cradled in his hands. Noah stood up, wiped the back of his jeans, and walked over to the friendless boy. He sat down on the ground beside him. Neither spoke to the other. Instead, they both sat on the narrow gravel shoulder, quietly holding on to dissimilar memories of home.

Chapter Thirteen

"HEY YOU! Hold up there! C'mere!" a large Indian boy shouted down the busy hall to a skinny Indian boy holding a bundle of books beneath one pencil-thin arm.

"Yeah, you. I wanna talk to you."

The skinny boy in thick-rimmed glasses looked around, frightened. He quickly ducked into the boy's bathroom and hid in a stall, pulling up his legs so they wouldn't be visible from outside the locked stall door. He sat quietly on the toilet, trembling. Then the bathroom door opened with a loud bang, and he heard footsteps echoing in the tiled room.

"I know you're in here, Brainiac. I just wanna talk to you."

The frightened boy held his stack of books tight against his thin chest, holding his breath, trying to meld with the porcelain and tile and plumbing.

The footsteps stopped in front of his stall. The terrified boy could see scuffed, brown shoes. Silence. Then a hard knock on the metal stall door.

"Come on. Open up. I know you're in there."

Silence again.

The skinny boy wondered how long he could hold his breath.

Then the shoes backed away from the door. A noise in the adjacent stall made the frightened boy look to his left, at the gray-steel wall of the compartment, just above the roll of toilet paper. The sound of a toilet seat lid dropped hard. Suddenly, a head appeared over the wall.

"You got my English paper, Brainiac?"

The scared boy didn't move. The Indian standing on the toilet of the adjoining stall leaned over until his face was directly over the other boy's cringing face. He let out a long, thick string of spittle, controlling it so that it slid slowly toward the weaker boy's face, thinning as it grew longer. Just as the spittle was about to land in the small boy's eye, he turned his face so that the spit landed on his hair, spilled over, and clung to his ear.

"You comin' outta there, or do I have to do it again?" the older, muscular boy asked, his voice full of the confidence that comes with size and age.

He hacked up another wad of spit, and just as it started its long, slow drip, the skinny boy burst out of his stall, trying to make it out the door.

"Help me!" he screamed, hoping people in the hallway would hear.

But he wasn't fast enough. The taller boy caught him, preventing his escape by blocking the door from opening with his foot. He gripped the skinny boy's collar in a fist and seized a shiny cigarette lighter from his pocket, flicked it open, and lit it, holding the tall flame close to the younger boy's face.

Without a word, the scrawny boy pulled a paper from between the pages of one of his books. Whimpering, he found a pencil in his shirt pocket and erased his own name from the top right-hand corner of the paper. He handed the nameless paper to the burly Indian, who slapped him hard on the side of his head. Before leaving the bathroom, the victorious thug spoke softly.

"See, Brainiac? All you gotta do is what you're told. It's that simple."

And that was less than ten minutes of one day.

Every school has its bullies. They are as ubiquitous as food fights in cafeterias, as kids smoking behind buildings. Some bullies are created by abusive parents—an alcoholic father who beats the hell out of his son because he hates his dead-end job; an indifferent and neglectful mother, strung out on booze and cigarettes and unfamiliar, broken men.

And some bullies are formed from other circumstances.

Back on his reservation, Philip Highmountain was big for his age, nevertheless, a kind and considerate boy, helpful and selfless. He had worked to collect canned food for a local food bank, always helped out at church when asked, and volunteered in the community whenever he had free time.

Everyone was proud of him.

"That boy's gonna be somebody," people would say.

"Why can't you be more like that Philip Highmountain?" parents would often scold wayward children.

Some children learned to deal with life at Wellington, steeling themselves against the neglect, the indifference, the denigration, the brutality. Some, like Noah, Simon, Lucy, and Elijah, had friends to help them endure the misery. Some collapsed under the pressure, like Arthur Pretty Shield. Over the years, Philip Highmountain's soul slowly corroded, like an iron ship at the bottom of a sunless sea, until what remained was ugly, twisted, and monstrous.

Phillip had lost himself at Wellington. At seventeen, nothing remained of the gentle-natured boy who had first passed beneath the rusted gate. He had converted. Now, he was the school terror, beating up other boys for any reason that struck him, molesting girls, taunting teachers, vandalizing property, and stealing from everyone. He had been arrested twice for stealing cars, and the police suspected him of breaking into the school's main office and taking money from a strong-box, but nothing was ever proven, the black strong-box never found.

Not even Dr. Dichter succeeded in catching Phillip in a clear-enough violation of school rules to punish him, as he so intensely wanted to do.

Highmountain was the boy Simon had bumped into in the cafeteria on the very first day of school. And Philip hadn't forgotten the encounter. Several times during the year he had caught Simon alone, giving him a black eye on one occasion. Generally, though, Simon was successful in simply running away.

Philip was trouble no matter how you slice it.

To make matters worse, he had a gang. Together, they ruthlessly intimidated the other students. More than bullies, Philip and his gang were the headmaster's enforcers. At his request, they meted out the school's less-than-legal punishments, like whipping younger boys.

One of their favorite victims was Arthur Pretty Shield. He was an easy target, smart in his subjects, always moping around, depressed, alone and friendless. Just about every week Arthur was beat up for something, sometimes simply for occupying the same space as Philip and his gang, for breathing the same air.

"This is for stinking up the place, you damn crybaby," they'd shout while punching him in the stomach or kicking him. Once, they actually broke one of his ribs. Arthur told the doctor he fell down the stairs, such was his fear of retaliation if he told the truth.

But their favorite victim was Charley Two Fists, a prideful little Apache, who was smaller than any of them but who always fought back, sometimes with unexpected success. His grandfather was a chief. Charley and Noah were friends, and they shared a class.

One night, after waiting down the hall for Charley's roommate to leave for the bathroom, Philip and several of his friends barged into Charley's dorm room. It was dark inside when they closed the door and began beating Charley. They certainly would have killed him had Charley not wriggled free and leaped out the three-story window. When his roommate returned, the door was ajar. Charley wasn't in his bed, and the window was shattered, a slight wind blowing the curtain. When the roommate looked out the window, he saw Charley lying on the cobblestone walk, all crumpled and twisted, blood seeping from his head, his teeth scattered on the walk like a pocketful of dice.

Charley died instantly.

He never had to fight for pride again.

The school buried him in the very last row of the nearly full cemetery, the cause of death listed in the local newspaper as an accident. Noah attended the hurried funeral. He read a poem and got goose bumps when they accidentally dropped the pine coffin into the grave, an arm dangling from the busted-open lid. Charley's tombstone read simply, "Two Fists, Apache."

The next day, a crow perched on the tombstone, cawing and cawing, until the groundskeeper chased it away.

No one saw who it was in the room that night. No one heard a thing. But everybody knew who it was. Charley's death was labeled accident, possibly a suicide—just one more lie in a parade of lies—and Philip Highmountain got away with murder.

ONLY TWO DAYS of school remained. Almost all of the students were staying for the summer. They would not leave Wellington until they graduated. For some that meant only a year or two. For others it meant many more years. One girl, Catherine Yassie, hadn't seen her folks in more than six years. Stricken with tuberculosis at the age of ten, her parents had taken her to a hospital, where, once cured after three months of treatment, she was sent straight to boarding school without getting to say goodbye to her family.

But a lucky few, those whose parents could afford it, would be allowed to go home for the summer. Those who stayed would be put to work, earning their keep at odd jobs around campus. Some would get low-wage jobs at local farms or orchards, picking vegetables or fruit. Noah and Elijah and a dozen other boys got jobs working as laborers for a construction company, carrying lumber for the builders and cleaning up the scraps, more go-fers than carpenters, despite their training.

Ever since the death of Lucy's mother, Simon's grandmother had been petitioning the government to allow her to act as Lucy's guardian. Even though she only knew Lucy from Simon's letters, she was determined to help her. Simon's grandmother organized cake walks and pancake breakfasts at church; she made dream-catchers and sold them to tourists. By summer vacation, she had raised enough money to bring both Simon and Lucy home.

Arthur Pretty Shield prayed that he'd get to go home, writing letters every week to his parents begging them to find a way so that he could go home. But in the end, they couldn't save him. Arthur would spend his allotted years at Wellington like the rest of the students too poor to see their families. School officials told Arthur that he'd spend the summer working in the laundry, one of the worst jobs of all. His worst nightmare realized, Arthur sank into an ever-deepening depression. He didn't speak to anyone. He didn't look at anyone. His mind was elsewhere, someplace dark and unfathomable. It had drowned beneath a hopeless sea, lying on its side on the mucky bottom alongside the wrecked hull of Philip Highmountain's soul. Arthur became the living dead, unable or unwilling to participate in the world of human interaction.

Something had to give.

On the last night of the school year, Elijah and Noah were walking across campus after supper. They had stayed so late that the kitchen staff kicked them out. It was dark when they passed the administration building.

Noah saw a figure climbing out a window.

"Hey," he said, pointing. "Isn't that Pretty Shield? What's he up to?"

They stopped and watched the shadowy figure running across the lawn, disappearing around the corner of the next building.

They didn't think much of it at the time. But fifteen minutes later, all hell broke loose. Sirens came screaming down the road, followed by fire trucks that pulled up alongside the administration building, which was on fire. Flames blazed out several windows on the ground floor. Students from nearby buildings gathered around the scene, firemen warning them to keep back.

Suddenly, the closest building lit up in flames too, its courtyard and nearby trees aglow. One of the fire trucks moved closer to combat the new fire. More and more students arrived, standing back a safe distance. No one said a word, every face expressing a strange ambiguity. No one was smiling, but no one was sad either. No one seemed concerned or worried. No one laughed and no one cried. All the young Indian faces reflected a blank stare, the flickering reddish-yellow light of the twin fires in their eyes. It was the look of indifference, as if they didn't care one way or the other—burn or not burn.

But then, quietly, as the fire burst out another window and set a nearby tree afire, one student began to clap, slowly. Another student joined in, matching the slow, methodical rhythm of the first. Then a dozen more and five dozen more, until every single Indian boy and girl was clapping in perfect harmony, the tempo increasing faster and faster, until eventually the synchronization fell apart and the night filled with the discordant sound of hundreds of hands clapping to their own time.

One boy, Arthur Pretty Shield, stood in the back row, alone as always. For the first time during the long year, he was smiling, tears streaming down his face. His clapping was the most enthusiastic of all.

Elijah and Noah exchanged glances, flashing big grins.

Both fires were contained during the long night. Neither building was destroyed. Wellington had survived, as inexorable, patient, as steadfast as winter, as certain as night. It prevailed. Made of everlasting stone and concrete and hardened commitment, it endured. Both buildings would be repaired before fall. The fires were only a small victory and a minor setback. But for one lonely, desperate boy, it was a victory nonetheless.

By morning, the fire trucks were gone. Inspectors quickly determined that both fires had been set purposefully. School officials even knew who did it. A shiny cigarette lighter was found at the source of the second fire with the initials *P. H.* scratched into the case. Dozens of other students, including a few gang members, identified the lighter.

It belonged to Philip Highmountain.

And by a strange and perfect coincidence, Philip had no alibi. He couldn't account for his whereabouts after supper. Truth is, he was out in the staff parking lot trying to steal a car, but the approaching sirens and flashing red lights in the darkness frightened him. Thinking the police were after him, he ran into the woods to hide. By noon, shouting his innocence, Highmountain was handcuffed and taken away in a black-and-white squad car. Hundreds of relieved and smiling children lined the driveway as the car drove down the hill and beneath the wrought iron gate, turning left at the highway. It was the last time anyone ever saw Philip Highmountain.

Revenge can be a beautiful thing, as warm and comforting as sunlight.

MISS CREGER ARRIVED at the headmaster's office at eleven a.m. to deliver her resignation letter in person, having made an appointment with his secretary the day before. Miss Creger had been to the headmaster's office before, and she remembered that there were two waiting chairs in front of the old gray-haired secretary's desk: a short one for children and a taller one for the older students and staff. But when she arrived punctually, only the child-size chair was sitting against the wall. For forty-five minutes she fidgeted uncomfortably in the tiny chair, feeling small and insignificant, listening to the secretary busily typing official daily forms.

Tak-tak-tak-tak.

In chorus with the grating sound of typing was the ticking of a large, round clock on the wall.

Tick-tick-tick-tick.

Miss Creger was developing a headache. Every time she interrupted the secretary to remind her that she had made an appointment, the response was the same.

"The headmaster's a very busy man," she'd reply dryly, without looking up from the typewriter. "I'm sure he'll be with you momentarily."

While she waited, Miss Creger rehearsed a prepared speech in her mind. In the speech, she wanted to say why she was leaving, how she had come to Wellington excited about the opportunity to inspire young minds, how she wanted to implement all the current teaching practices and strategies she had learned at college. She wanted to tell the headmaster how the school had crushed all her hopes and enthusiasm, how it was broke and needed repair, how she just couldn't be part of it any longer. She expected to have a productive discussion about the problems with the school's policies and their remedies, especially about the various uses of punishment. She would specifically cite the cruel imprisonment of Simon Lone Fight, being careful not to disclose that it was she who had written the anonymous letter threatening to contact the police. She would speak to apathetic teachers and to bullying and abuse and about creating a more nurturing environment. She even had a couple quotes she planned to use to support her argument, sayings such as *Minds are like fires that must be kindled by curiosity* and *Kindness begets kindness.*

Finally, at a quarter to noon, Miss Creger was called in to Dr. Dichter's office. Without ceremony she handed him her letter in an envelope. The headmaster barely glanced at the letter before sliding it back into the envelope.

"Good day, Miss Creger," he said, as he turned around in his leather chair so that his back was to the anxious, young teacher.

"But I wanted to talk to you about . . ."

"I said good day!" he snapped, without turning around.

This wasn't the first time Dr. Dichter had received a teacher's resignation in such a manner. At the end of every school year, it seemed, some young, sympathetic, and idealistic teacher came to see him with resignation letter in hand. He prided himself for being able to ascertain which new teacher it would be. In the early years as headmaster, he sat and listened respectfully to the litany of concerns and complaints. But over the years, he had grown weary and intolerant, and he now embraced a policy of stifling the rants before they even began. Such monologues accomplished nothing, he had decided. They were a waste of his time. If it was up to him, and it was, none of the school's policies were going to change. Not a one.

Nothing ever changed at Wellington.

As Miss Creger left the headmaster's office, the thin, gray-haired secretary, still sitting behind her desk, held out a white envelope.

"Dr. Dichter instructed me to give this to you when you left his office," she said.

Miss Creger opened it. Inside was her final paycheck.

It was dated the day before.

As the disillusioned teacher left the school, walking past the cemetery, her dainty shoes clicking on the cobbled sidewalk, she wondered how many of the children's heart-torn hopes and dreams would end up buried there. With her face wet from tears, Miss Creger walked beneath the wrought iron gate.

THAT AFTERNOON, Noah and Elijah walked with Simon and Lucy to the train stop. Low clouds overhead threatened rain. On the way, they all promised how they would write to one another all summer.

"And ask your grandmother to send a box of fry bread," Elijah requested, almost begging. That's one of the many things he missed about home, the taste of good fry bread, the smell of it filling the house.

"You keep an eye on Lucy, and make sure nothing happens to her," Noah said, shaking a finger at Simon, scolding him like an old lady.

"Yeah, yeah. Don't worry, Mom," replied Simon, smiling down at Lucy, who was holding a small, plaid suitcase she had borrowed from another girl who was not going home.

The four of them stood on the platform waiting for the train, which arrived five minutes late. When it came to a full stop, they said their farewells and hugged, as a few other Indian children boarded the west-bound train. Most of them had no one with whom to share good-byes.

"I'll see you in the fall."

"Stay out of trouble."

"I'll think about you every day."

"I promise, I'll write."

"Don't get lost on the way home."

"Take care of each other."

"Thanks for everything."

It was drizzling when Simon and Lucy boarded the train and handed their tickets to the porter. From the small platform, Noah and Elijah watched as their friends found a seat and waved at them from a window. A few minutes later, a shrill whistle blew and, with a clanking jolt, the train pulled away. Noah and Elijah stood on the empty platform and watched until the train and their friends vanished around a curve, then they walked back to the school in silence, both longing to be going home.

Rain was pouring down by the time they passed beneath the school gate. Aboard the warm train, Lucy and Simon were weeping silently, and neither knew why for sure. For the next several hours, the two friends quietly played cards, each lost in thought and occasionally looking out the rain-streaked window at the passing world. Every minute aboard the rattling train carried Simon and Lucy another mile toward home—and a million miles away from Wellington.

Epilogue

AND ALTHOUGH THE FIRST YEAR at Wellington turned into memory, the way all moments and years must, no matter how joyous or dreadful, other years followed the way spring follows winter and dawn follows night. For Noah, Simon, and Elijah, three more years came and went before they left for home. For Lucy, four more years passed. Without her friends, the last was the hardest and loneliest. In between, most students graduated and returned to wherever they were from, to where it was they had once called home: to north or west, east or south. Some did not return home; they simply left Wellington, left everything, ran away. Either way, their departures emptied beds for new arrivals to take their place.

Indian out, Indian in—forever new, forever the same, a relentless machinery that lasted for almost a hundred years.

A story such as this one can have no happy ending, no tidy or joyful resolution, no coming-of-age or lessons learned. There were none. Too many lives were impacted and irrevocably changed. The lost years could not be recovered; the lost identities could not be restored. Many of the children who returned home after graduation were never fully accepted as Indian. And though it had not been their choice to go the boarding schools, some became outcasts, not so much for anything they had done, but because of what they represented: the dissolution of Indian identity.

For the most part, the schools stripped the children of their Indian heritage, but it failed miserably to replace that heritage with the promised new one. Neither white nor fully Indian, the stolen generation grew into adulthood, rambling through life as best they could—as we all must—without a clear sense of identity, never fully fitting in anywhere.

The endings were all the same, more or less, differing in their sadness only by degree. At best it can be said that some stories were less harsh, some more. And the children weren't the only ones harmed. The despondent parents were affected by the absence of their children, as were siblings by the absence of brother or sister. Even the eventual offspring of the children would be affected. How does one love others when no love was afforded to them?

And what of the community?

There was no community resolution.

Stories such as this can end only one way—by telling how it ended for each of the children, one story at a time—one shattered life at a time.

DURING HIS LAST YEARS AT WELLINGTON, Elijah learned to stop seeing ghosts. Relentlessly, in every classroom and on every wall, the teachers instructed the children that Indian beliefs and customs, like their primitive languages, are old-fashioned and based on superstition. They said it so often, drummed it into their brains so consistently, that many of the children believed it, saw their own families—without telephones or televisions, without dishwashers or vacuum cleaners—as antiquated and embarrassing.

Whenever the ghosts came to visit, Elijah learned to close his eyes, telling them to go away, ignoring them. They were part of the past, the way the dead always are. Sometimes he counted to one hundred before opening his eyes, squinting first to see if they were still there. For a long time they kept coming, following him around the school, desperate and pleading, despite the boy's attempts to ignore them. But eventually they stopped coming altogether, leaving Elijah's spirit as barren as a ghost.

A piece of who he was had been removed, a part as essential as his heart.

When Elijah returned home, the spirits returned, drawn by whatever mysterious force that draws them. Even Elijah didn't know how to explain it. He had no one to talk to about it. His grandfather, the chief, had died while he was away.

Full of questions he could not answer, Elijah never forgot his grandfather's warning that the power to see the dead can use up a weak man.

"Not every man can carry the gift," he had said that day while changing the tire.

In an effort to drown out the images, Elijah began to drown himself. As with so many of the countless children stolen from their homes and families, taken from the soil in their flesh, the bottle gave him temporary respite. Some say alcohol makes you forget. For Elijah, it made him remember. He remembered how things used to be, his place in the world, in life, in nature. And the recollection of something so utterly and completely lost tore a hole in him so great he could put his fist through it.

Year after year, lonely as an abandoned cemetery, Elijah drowned out everything and everyone, spirit and living alike, until he became a ghost.

LIKE ELIJAH, NOAH RETURNED TO HIS VILLAGE four years older than when he left, able to multiply and divide; knowledgeable of commas, nouns, adverbs, and prepositional phrases; aware of the capitol of every state and where to find other nations on a map. He even knew what stars are made of and how to tie a Windsor knot and how to read Latin poorly. But Noah no longer felt himself a part of the land.

187

No matter how hard he tried, he never fit in.

"You're not one of us anymore," proclaimed the other men, turning their backs on Noah because they felt he had turned his back on them.

It didn't occur to them that Noah had no choice, that his folks had no choice. They failed to realize that it could just as easily have been their son or daughter taken away, even themselves, had they been younger.

Though he was a handsome young man, none of the young women in the village would go out with him. Their parents forbade them from getting involved with the misfit, concerned that Noah's shame at having been transformed into something foreign would rub off on them like a contagion.

"He's more white man than Indian," mothers and fathers warned their daughters.

Noah Boyscout was neither here nor there, a disembodied shadow looking for someone to claim it, lonesome as an Arctic tern spanning a tempestuous sea.

After years of trying to fit in, Noah built a cabin several miles downriver from the small village, not to find his place in nature as he had once done, but to find relief from the contempt of neighbors and relatives. No one came to visit, except for ravens, squirrels, and the occasional bear. He spent his lonely days cutting and hauling firewood, running trap lines far into the hills, hunting moose and caribou, snaring rabbits and shooting ducks, catching enough salmon to feed his sled dogs, only going into the village to trade pelts for the things the land did not provide.

Whereas Noah had once found solace in the wilderness, now he found mostly loneliness. The land does not provide friendship or love, only hardship.

The people of his tribe abandoned Noah the way some animals desert their newborn when handled by man.

THE YEARS AT WELLINGTON passed slowly for Simon, like a desert tortoise struggling to flee a grass fire, the way wind and sand erode stone, the way moving water furrows bedrock. He became like a tumbleweed, a dry husk spinning aimlessly on the wind.

As magnificently defiant as he had once been, Simon simply gave up, somehow losing the second word in his surname. By the time he left Wellington, there was no fight left in him. He no longer remembered the beautiful language of his grandmother and grandfather. He no longer dreamed in the words of his ancestors, the words for which he had been so eager to be chained and shamed. The legend of his previous courage would survive, as much a part of the institution as the bricks themselves, but the spark of Simon's resistance was extinguished, the love of running was quieted, as if a heavy rain had drenched his soul until it trembled from cold, turned soggy, and fell apart as if made of cardboard.

Even the greatest tree one day loses its footing and falls to the forest floor, followed by an awesome, lasting silence.

Simon returned to Four Corners after his graduation, clutching the diploma that said he was an educated citizen of the world's greatest nation, a proud nation born from the escape of religious persecution, a nation anchored in individual freedom. He moved into a small, silver trailer on concrete blocks on a barren hill overlooking a valley five miles from his old town, his only neighbors jack rabbits, lizards, snakes, scorpions, and stones. All summer long the hot desert sun baked Simon inside his tinny home like a loaf of bread in a horno.

Over several years Simon worked a number of odd jobs: the gas station, the bingo parlor, the mini-golf. He even sold insurance door-to-door for a while. He never sold a single policy. Other Indians simply looked at him as he stood in their doorway, wearing a suit and tie with his briefcase and hat in hand. They stared at him, puzzled by his sales pitch, wondering how one is insured against the future.

Through it all, the Wellington diploma hung from Simon's refrigerator door like a paper tongue mocking him. The years at Wellington had changed Simon, but it hadn't changed how America looked at him or at any of the other Indians with similar diplomas.

One day, Simon built a funeral pyre. He stripped off his suit jacket, white dress shirt and tie, kicked off his trousers and shiny black shoes, and cremated them along with his diploma and the briefcase full of brochures. Simon ran deep into the arroyos, mesas, and canyons, running along red buttes and dry creek beds lined with desert flowers and sage brush, pushed along by the raging storm of an unfulfilled promise.

Simon ran so far and so fast that he finally lost his exhausted shadow.

He built a hogan, a sweat lodge, and a corral made from piñon trees and thorn bushes. He grew corn and raised sheep amid the loneliness and the beauty, where antelope sometimes grazed among his sheep. From elders, he slowly relearned everything Wellington had taken from him. There in the wilderness, one stolen piece at a time, Simon reclaimed himself, eventually becoming an Indian activist and a respected tribal leader, a beacon of Indian pride as bright as any bonfire.

THE YOUNGEST OF THE FOUR, LUCY stayed at Wellington the longest. The extra year she endured allowed the school's insidious messages to take root more deeply into the shallow soil of her self.

English Only!

No Indian Dancing!

When Lucy returned to her small village, she went to see the small cabin where she and her mother had lived, where they had sung in the sauna, eaten rabbit soup, combed out each other's long hair before bed. The old cabin, like her mother, was gone, burned to the ground by vandals. Dandelion and fireweed grew in the emptiness where the house once stood. A spruce sapling took root where their bed used to be.

Nothing of Lucy's past remained. Only the constant stars and the northern lights reminded her of what had been.

All alone, outcast and confused, with the slogans of Wellington forever rattling in her mind, Lucy embraced the modern world, living in cities, owning televisions and vacuum cleaners, and eventually using cell phones, flying on jet planes, shopping at supermarts and, eventually, at glistening mega-malls, and watching movies at the Cineplex. Little by little, one word at a time, she forgot much of the language in which she and her mother used to tell each other stories.

Lucy married white men, three times, her five half-breed children marrying whites as well, until she no longer saw herself or her mother in the faces of her grandchildren or great grandchildren, until one day when she was very old, one of her grandsons with light hair and blue eyes—one of the only ones left who could still recite the old myths and speak her old language—would tell her stories. . . .

Including this one.

Questions for Discussion

1. The residential Indian boarding school experiment lasted from 1879 until about 1960, though it was winding down by the mid-1950s. The schools were built to be places that would utterly transform Indian people, obliterating tribal identity, destroying Native languages, and eradicating Native religions, customs, and traditions. The stated idea behind the policy was to "Kill the Indian to save the man." At its height, there were 153 of these schools in America. Parallel histories exist in Canada's treatment of First Nations people as well as in Australia's dealings with Aboriginals. Nowadays, Australia has a national "Sorry Day" to recognize the wrongs committed against aboriginal peoples. What do you think of the policy? Can you think of a better way to bring American Indians into mainstream American culture? Was it even necessary?

2. It is a sad fact that in the early years, thousands of Indian children died from diseases to which they had no previous immunity, especially from trachoma, influenza, and tuberculosis. The government blamed the epidemic on the Indians' physical inferiority, insisting they had brought it upon themselves. Do you think that was true? Does anyone deserve to be treated the way these Indian children were treated?

3. Wellington is not based on a single institution. It is an amalgamation of schools, symbolic of the boarding school experience. Discuss the irony of the school's name, Wellington, and the students' nickname for it.

4. It is a historical fact that handcuffs were used on the children, sometimes as young as six or seven, especially during initial apprehension and transportation to the schools. The practice seems to have ended before the 1950s. Haskell Indian Nations University (formerly Haskell Indian School) in Lawrence, Kansas has a pair of handcuffs used on Indian children on display in their Cultural Center and Museum. You can see them on their website.

5. Almost immediately, boys received haircuts (girls with excessively long hair also had their hair cut). Why do you think the schools did that first thing?

6. Which character(s) do you most identify with or sympathize with and why?

7. In many ways, Miss Creger is the most sympathetic teacher, a voice of conscience. But in the end, she resigns from Wellington. Why did she leave? Could she have made a difference if she stayed?

8. The author of this novel interviewed over a hundred Indian elders nationwide as part of his research for this book. Indeed, many of his own relatives attended Indian boarding schools. Few elders ever speak of their experiences. In recent decades, stories have surfaced of rampant child abuse and pedophilia at the schools. So far from home, and without family to protect them, Indian children fell victim to predators,

and the victims themselves often became victimizers. Discuss why this may be so.

9. As incredulous as they may seem, all of the events in the novel (Simon's imprisonment, sexual abuse by teachers, the wolf attack on Noah, Lucy's abduction, the incident on the bus, ghost stories, Elijah's shamanistic awakening, etc.) come from actual events and interviews with elders. Does knowing these events were true affect your reaction to the book?

10. Some readers have suggested that it was good that the government took Lucy away from her mother and their life of poverty, even though there was a lot of love. Is it right for the government to remove children from families simply because they are poor? If your family fell on hard times, would you want to be taken away?

11. In many ways, boarding schools were the destruction of the Indian family. From years away from family and without love and affection afforded to them, many children grew up unable to show love when they eventually had families of their own. Discuss how our personality is influenced by past experiences, especially during the formative years of childhood and adolescence.

12. The image of the school gate is a recurring theme. What is the function of the gate in the story?

13. Why is language so important in this novel? How are language and culture interconnected?

14. As a class, watch the movie Rabbit Proof Fence. Although set in Australia, there are many parallels.

15. As a class project, research several Indian reservations or villages. In groups, present your findings, include photographs, video, and socioeconomic statistics as a virtual tour of contemporary reservation life.

16. The manuscript of this novel languished in a desk drawer for a decade because agents and publishers said the story was too depressing. They wanted a happy ending to ease their conscience. But a happy ending would be a disservice to the generations of Indian children who were stolen from their families and subjected to these institutions. Winston Groom, the author of Forrest Gump, tried to convince the author not to publish it, saying "it would give America a black eye." But great stories, especially those based on history, can't always have happy endings. Yet, the stories need to be told nonetheless. We can't know who we are as a people and as a nation until we know the truth about where we came from. Abraham Lincoln once wrote that "history is not history unless it is the truth." Do you think this story needed to be told? Do you think it's important? Has your understanding of American history changed? What do you gain from such awareness?

The Stealing Indians
Oral History Project

One of the enduring objectives for this book was to create a national archive of narratives from American Indians and Canadian First Nation Natives who attended boarding schools. The stated purpose of the project is to make the narratives available to the public in an effort to document the true history of America and Canada. If you or anyone in your family—a parent or grandparent, aunt or uncle, cousin or second cousin, brother or sister—would like to share their recollections of their experience at boarding school, or if they told them to you in the past or recorded them, please submit the story in any format: as an email, word doc, letter, or even as an audio or video recording that can be transcribed. To learn how to participate, email stealingindiansproject@gmail.com

The Author

John Smelcer is the author of fifty books. His books of mythology include *In the Shadows of Mountains*, *The Raven and the Totem* (introduced by Joseph Campbell), and *A Cycle of Myths*. In 1994, he co-edited the acclaimed anthology *Durable Breath: Contemporary Native American Poetry*. His writing has appeared in over 400 magazines and journals worldwide, including in *The Atlantic*.

The son of an Alaska Native father, John served as executive director of his tribe's Heritage Foundation, compiling and editing *The Ahtna Noun Dictionary and Pronunciation Guide* (forewords by Noam Chomsky and Steven Pinker). As of the writing of this biography, John is the last living tribal member who can read, write, and speak Ahtna. For four years he served as the director of Chenega Native Corporation's Language and Cultural Preservation Project, working with elders to compile *The Alutiiq Noun Dictionary and Pronunciation Guide* (foreword by H. H. The Dalai Lama) and editing *The Day That Cries Forever* and *We are the Land, We are the Sea*. In 1999, Ahtna Chief Harry Johns designated John a Traditional Culture Bearer, awarding him the necklaces of the late Chief Jim McKinley. That same year, John was nominated for the Alaska Governor's Award for his preservation of Alaska Native languages and cultures. In 2013, John was recommended to The White House to receive the Presidential Citizen's Medal for his efforts to preserve America's Native heritage.

John Smelcer has written over a dozen books of poetry, including *Indian Giver, Changing Seasons, Songs from an Outcast,*

Without Reservation (winner of the 2004 Western Writers of America Spur Award for Poetry and Binghamton University's 2004 Kessler Prize for Poetry), *The Binghamton Poems* (edited by John Updike), *Tracks, Raven Speaks* (foreword by Ted Hughes), *Riversongs*, and numerous bilingual volumes including, *Beautiful Words, The Indian Prophet,* and *The Language Raven Gave Us.* In the early 1990s, Allen Ginsberg called John "one of the most brilliant younger poets in America."

John Smelcer's first novel, *The Trap*, received the James Jones Prize for the First Novel and was named a Notable Book by the American Library Association and the New York Public Library. A review in England hailed it "the most haunting and best written book of the year." *The Trap* is listed among the 101 greatest novels to teach the English language worldwide. His follow-up novel, *The Great Death*, also published in the U.S. and the U.K., was listed as one of the greatest adventure stories of all time. John's novel *Edge of Nowhere* was listed as one of the ten best YA novels in 2014. In the UK, it was hailed as the book to challenge *Robinson Crusoe*'s place in the survival genre. John's mountain climbing novel, *Savage Mountain*, is based on true events. With Joseph Bruchac, John co-edited *Native American Classics,* hailed as one of the hottest graphic novels of 2013. Aside from a Ph.D. in English and creative writing, John's education includes post-doctoral studies at Cambridge, Oxford, and Harvard.

Links

Visit Leapfrog Press on Facebook
Google: Facebook Leapfrog Press
or enter:
https://www.facebook.com/pages/Leapfrog-Press/222784181103418

Leapfrog Press Website
www.leapfrogpress.com

Author Website
www.johnsmelcer.com

CPSIA information can be obtained
at www.ICGtesting.com
Printed in the USA
FSOW02n0813010316
17421FS